Art Klutz

Then Patti turned to me. "How about you, Lauren? What do you think you'll do for the art fair?"

"I'm still not sure," I confessed. Why couldn't jogging or shooting baskets be on the list of projects?

Kate said, "Lauren, we'll help you."

Stephanie frowned. "Why would Lauren need our help? She's got more imagination than any of us."

I couldn't help thinking they were wrong. I was the biggest art klutz in the whole school, and soon everyone was going to know it.

Look for these and other books
in the Sleepover Friends Series:

Lauren's Double Disaster

Susan Saunders

AN
APPLE
PAPERBACK

SCHOLASTIC INC.
New York Toronto London Auckland Sydney

ISBN 0-590-43926-X

Copyright © 1991 by Daniel Weiss Associates, Inc. All rights reserved. Published by Scholastic Inc. APPLE PAPERBACKS is a registered trademark of Scholastic Inc. SLEEPOVER FRIENDS is a registered trademark of Daniel Weiss Associates, Inc.

12 11 10 9 8 7 6 5 4 3 2 1   1 2 3 4 5 6/9

Printed in the U.S.A.   28

First Scholastic printing, February 1991

Chapter
1

"I've got a million ideas already," Kate Beekman said when we were on our way to lunch that Friday. "This art fair is going to be terrific!"

Kate plans to be a famous film director someday. She's already won a contest at a local television station with one of her videos — starring the Sleepover Friends! (That's me, Lauren Hunter, plus Patti Jenkins and Stephanie Green.) So it wasn't surprising that Kate was excited. To her, this was another chance to show her talent and win a prize, even if it's only a ribbon.

Our teacher, Mrs. Mead, had told us all about it in class that morning. The same old art fair that Riverhurst Elementary has every year was going to be even worse than usual this year, as far as I was concerned. All the students' artworks were going to be auctioned off to benefit a children's hospital.

"What if no one buys our work?" I asked nervously.

"No problem," Kate said as Patti and Stephanie joined us in the lunchline. "Everyone knows that our parents will buy everything."

"Really?" I asked. That made me feel a little better. Surely my own parents couldn't refuse to buy my artwork — no matter how bad it was. And it was usually pretty bad. Trust me. I know what I'm talking about.

"That does make sense," Patti said. She sounded relieved, too. Patti's almost as bad at art as I am.

"Of course, some famous film producer *might* stop by the art auction and decide to buy my project as an investment in the future of the industry," Kate said grandly as we shuffled forward in the slow-moving line.

"You're joking, aren't you?" Stephanie asked suspiciously. Stephanie thinks that Kate can be a little pompous sometimes. But Kate *is* good at what she does. It isn't too hard to imagine something like that really happening to her.

That just goes to show how different Kate and I are. It's not just that Kate's artistic and I'm not. I mean, I'm tall, and she's short. I have medium brown hair and hazel eyes, Kate is a blue-eyed blonde. I'm easygoing, Kate isn't. The list goes on and on.

When you stop to think about it, it's amazing

that Kate and I are friends at all. And we're *best* friends, and have been practically our whole lives. The Beekmans have an old photograph of Kate and me as babies to prove it. We're sitting on a blanket grinning at each other, wearing nothing but diapers.

It was Kate and I who first started having sleep-overs when we were in kindergarten. We had so many sleepovers, Kate's dad named us the Sleepover Twins. And we were the Sleepover Twins right up until Stephanie moved to Riverhurst last year from the city, and was in my class. After a less than perfect beginning — Kate and Stephanie refused to get along at first — the Sleepover Twins turned into the Sleep-over Trio.

Then, at the beginning of this year, Patti walked into our class, 5B. Stephanie was thrilled because Patti was also from the city. Patti and Stephanie had even gone to the same school in first grade, and they already knew each other, sort of. Anyway, Stephanie liked Patti, and so did Kate and I — she's one of the nicest people I've ever met. Now, we're the *four* Sleepover Friends, and we have sleepovers almost every Friday night. I can't imagine things being any other way!

"What do you think you'll do, Lauren?" Kate asked as we started putting food on our trays.

"I guess I'll have to wait until I see what Ms. Gilberto suggests this afternoon." Ms. Gilberto is our art teacher. I took some red Jell-O with fruit in it and a hot dog. "I'm not exactly bursting with great artistic ideas," I confessed.

"Don't worry, Lauren," Kate said. "Stephanie, Patti, and I will help you come up with something good."

I smiled. Being one of the four Sleepover Friends meant having three best friends who would do just about anything for you!

"I hope fashion design is on Ms. Gilberto's list," Stephanie said. She took a carton of milk and led the way to our favorite table. Stephanie's a great artist — besides drawing and painting, she's also a terrific clothes designer. The art fair would be no problem for her.

"How about you, Patti?" I asked. "Have you got any ideas yet?"

"Not yet," said Patti. "I'm not even going to think about it until art class." She picked up her hot dog and took a bite.

"That's how I feel," I said. At least I wasn't the only one without an idea. I was glad Patti wasn't an art genius.

"What are you going to think about if you aren't going to think about the art fair, Patti?" teased Kate. "Henry, perhaps?" The rest of us snickered a little. Patti sits next to Henry Larkin in Mrs. Mead's class, and they have a crush on each other. On Valentine's

Day, Patti and Henry had sort of gone public — they actually danced together in front of everyone at our Valentine's Day sock hop! We love to tease Patti about it.

Patti blushed. "Nooo," she said. "I'm thinking about the sleepover at my house tonight, of course. Has everyone got together her contribution to the Italian potluck?" Patti had planned a special Italian dinner, and we were each supposed to bring something.

"My mom's making the Italian bread from scratch," Stephanie announced. "I told her she didn't have to go to all that trouble, but she said she wanted to. She's making a batch of her cookies for us, too." Mrs. Green has her hands full with Stephanie's twin brother and sister, but she still tries to do special things for Stephanie.

"My salad is going to have a little bit of everything in it," I promised, mostly because I hadn't decided on the specifics yet. But how hard could it be to make salad?

"How about you, Kate?" Patti asked. "Have you got dessert under control?"

"Totally. But I'm not telling you what it is — you'll have to wait until tonight to find out. I *will* say it's really special, though," Kate said mysteriously.

"Hi! Mind if I sit with you?" Hope Lenski was

standing next to our table holding her bag lunch.

"Of course not," Patti said. She patted the empty chair next to her and Hope sat down.

Hope is the newest girl in Mrs. Mead's class, and we've become pretty friendly with her. After Patti, she's one of the nicest people I've ever met. She brings her own lunch every day because she's a vegetarian, which means she doesn't eat anything with meat in it, like hot dogs. And that's not the only thing unusual about her. Sometimes she wears what I think are kind of strange combinations of clothes, like Indian-print skirts and tie-dyed shirts. She also likes to make tons of little braids in her long blonde hair.

Hope looked around and smiled at all of us. "Isn't the art fair exciting?" she asked.

I groaned silently. All I wanted to do was forget about it . . . for now at least!

"What are you thinking about doing, Hope?" Kate asked. She yanked off a grape and popped it into her mouth.

Hope was unwrapping her sandwich. "Something in fiber arts," she said.

"Fiber arts?" I repeated. I couldn't help giggling a little. "That sounds like some kind of health food diet."

Hope tried not to laugh — her mouth was full of sandwich. Finally she said, "Fiber arts is stuff like weaving, quilting, and needlepoint."

"Oh," I said. I felt like even more of an art klutz now.

"I have my own loom," Hope added. "My dad made it for me."

"Really?" Stephanie asked. "I'd really like to see your loom sometime. Different textures of fabric would make an interesting fashion statement. That's what I'm doing for the fair — fashion design."

"You can all come over and see the loom if you want," Hope said. "I'll have to check with my dad to find out which day is best for him — then I'll let you know." Hope's dad is a veterinarian, and his clinic is attached to their house. I'm sure he wouldn't want a bunch of girls running around while he was trying to get a cat to say, "Ah."

"Great!" everybody but me said. It wasn't that I didn't want to see Hope's loom. I just didn't want to think about the art fair anymore. At least not now — maybe not *ever*. For the first time in my life, I wasn't looking forward to the first day of spring.

After lunch, we have recess. On Mondays, Wednesdays, and Fridays after recess, we have art.

Ms. Gilberto started art class that Friday with a discussion of the upcoming art fair. Since Mrs. Mead had already told us almost everything, Ms. Gilberto jumped right to the question part. Of course, Karla

Stamos's hand shot right up. Karla is the class grind. Her favorite color is brown, and her greatest ambition is to be the teacher's pet. You can just imagine what her personality is like.

"Yes, Karla?" Ms. Gilberto said.

"How many projects can we enter, Ms. Gilberto?" Karla asked.

Kate and I looked at each other and shook our heads.

"Just one, Karla," Ms. Gilberto said. "You only have two weeks, and that's not enough time to do more than one really special project, is it?"

Karla shook her head, looking disappointed.

Next, Hope asked if she could work at home. Ms. Gilberto said that we'd definitely have to work at home since there was so little time.

Then Ms. Gilberto handed out lists of suggestions. Henry Larkin, Mark Freedman, and a bunch of other boys immediately started making their lists into paper airplanes. When Ms. Gilberto ignored them, they actually started flying them across the room. It was outrageous. Things like that never happen in Mrs. Mead's class, but Ms. Gilberto isn't very good at discipline.

Finally, Ms. Gilberto gave up trying to lead an orderly discussion and told us we could use the rest of our class time to talk over our ideas with each other. She said she would make herself available if we needed her. Then she buried her head in an art book and ignored the chaos that followed. At least I wouldn't have to do any art at all that day.

"Now I know what I'm going to do," Patti announced as soon as the four of us had gathered around a table in the corner, out of the way of the boys' paper airplanes. "Something to do with computer graphics."

"Really?" Kate sounded skeptical. "Drawing on a computer is art?"

Obviously, Kate had quit looking at Ms. Gilberto's list as soon as she'd spotted photography and film. I, on the other hand, had read the list all the way through — twice. Computer graphics was definitely there, and I was definitely in trouble. Patti sounded as inspired as Kate and Stephanie were! Now I was the only one of the Sleepover Friends who wasn't excited.

Patti nodded. "Do you remember that movie my parents took Horace and me to see at the science museum in the city last month?" Horace is Patti's little brother. "All the animation for it was done with a computer." Patti was sounding more enthusiastic by the minute. It was really depressing. "If I learn more about how that movie was made, I might be able to do something like it —

9

but on a smaller scale, of course."

Then Patti turned to me. "How about you, Lauren? Which category do you think you'll do?"

"I'm still not sure," I confessed. Why couldn't jogging or shooting baskets be on the list? Those were the things *I* liked.

Kate said, "Like I told you before lunch, Lauren, we'll help you."

Stephanie frowned. "Why would Lauren need *our* help? She's got more imagination than any of us."

Kate chuckled. "That's true." Kate likes to say I have a runaway imagination. She also likes to tell me to get a grip on it.

"There's plenty to choose from," Stephanie declared. She picked up the list and started reading it. "Painting, drawing, sculpture, *fashion design*."

"There's *too* much," I said, before she could rattle off any more categories. "And I'm not exactly — " I began. But before I could explain that having a vivid imagination didn't necessarily mean I was an artist, the bell rang.

"That's it for today, boys and girls," Ms. Gilberto said with a relieved smile. "I'll be here from now until the art fair if any of you need any help. Meanwhile, please remember that there's a way for *everyone* to express themselves through art."

As I trudged back to 5B, I couldn't help thinking Ms. Gilberto was wrong. There was a way for *almost* everyone to express themselves through art — everyone but me! Lauren Hunter was the biggest art klutz in the whole school, and soon everyone was going to know it.

Chapter
2

My brother Roger drove me to Patti's house Friday night. He's seventeen and has his own car. He's usually pretty nice about driving me places, but he's always in a hurry. That night he had a dinner date with his girlfriend Linda.

"Don't forget your salad," he said as I got out of the car. He drummed his thumbs nervously on the steering wheel.

"I don't think I can carry it all. At least, not all at once," I said. I had my overnight bag, too.

"Then take the salad in first, and come back for your other junk," he said. "I have to go, Lauren. I don't want to keep Linda waiting."

"Okay, okay," I said. I set my overnight stuff down on the driveway. Then I picked up the salad bowl and bumped the car door shut with my hip. Roger started backing out of the Jenkins' driveway.

I had to quickly kick my bag out of the way or he would have run right over it.

I walked to the front door with the salad and rang the bell. A few seconds later, Patti's little brother Horace opened the door.

"Come on in," Horace said. He's only six, but most of the time he seems older than that because he's really smart. He recently skipped up into second grade.

"Hi, Horace," I said as I stepped inside. I saw both Kate's and Stephanie's overnight bags at the foot of the stairs.

"Oh, hi, Lauren," Mrs. Jenkins said, coming out from the study. "I thought I heard the doorbell. The other girls are out in the kitchen."

"Thanks, Mrs. Jenkins," I said.

"We'll have our dessert after the girls are through with the kitchen," I heard Mrs. Jenkins promising Horace. "Meanwhile, I want you to finish cleaning those cages like you promised."

Horace has a horrible collection of pets, including a snake, two turtles, an ant farm, a salamander, and several hermit crabs. I'm glad we have a regular pet — a dog. Even though Bullwinkle weighs 130 pounds and is a lot of dog to handle, living with him is definitely better than living with a snake!

Suddenly the door to the kitchen flew open.

"There you are!" Kate cried. She raised one eyebrow. "You're late, Lauren." Kate, of course, is never late. She's too organized for that.

Mrs. Jenkins laughed. "Enjoy your dinner, girls," she said. She went back into the study and closed the door.

I looked at Kate and wrinkled up my nose. "Thinking about Horace's creepy crawlies has ruined my appetite," I told her.

Kate laughed. "Your appetite — ruined? Impossible."

I smiled, and socked Kate playfully in the arm. She's always teasing me about my healthy appetite.

In the kitchen, the table was already set. There was a red-and-white-checkered tablecloth and matching napkins. In the center of the table was a green bottle with a red candle stuck in it. The bottle was surrounded by bunches of fake grapes.

"Very Italian," I said appreciatively. "This was a great idea, Patti."

"Thanks," Patti said. "I got the idea from a dinner party my parents had. This was their centerpiece."

"I like it," I told her. I pulled the tin foil off the salad bowl.

Just then the back door opened and Patti's father walked in. "Does this belong to one of you?" he said, holding up my green-and-purple-striped tote.

"Oh, that's mine!" I cried. "I guess I forgot it outside. Thanks, Mr. Jenkins."

Mr. Jenkins handed it to me. "No problem. I'm glad nothing happened to it." He smiled and left the kitchen.

"Laur-en," Kate said.

"Don't say it! Anyway, I had too much to carry," I said defending myself.

"Okay," Patti said, to change the subject. She was standing over a large steaming pot on the stove. "The pasta is ready." She held up one long, skinny, limp noodle as evidence and my stomach growled excitedly. Kate had been right. It took more than Horace's pets to kill *my* appetite!

The next few minutes were taken up with filling our four plates with spaghetti, salad, and the hot buttered Italian bread that Stephanie's mom had made. But as soon as we were sitting down, just what I'd been hoping wouldn't happen *did* happen. The conversation turned to the art fair.

"I've already started doing some sketches for my fashion design," Stephanie said as she twirled spaghetti onto her fork. "I don't like to brag, but I think my project is going to be fabulous. How about the rest of you?"

"I've narrowed down my ideas a little bit," Kate said. "But I'm having trouble pinpointing exactly what I should do. Two weeks isn't a lot of time to

15

do something really good, and I want my project to be the best.''

"I wanted to go back to the science museum and see that computer animation film again,'' Patti said. "But unfortunately the film isn't being shown there anymore. I guess I'll have to go to the library and see if I can find anything on computer animation there. If I can't, I might have to think of something else to do. It's definitely going to be something to do with computer graphics, though.''

No one seemed to notice that I wasn't saying anything. But what could I say? They were all charged with ideas and enthusiasm, and I wasn't. About all I could do was complain, and I didn't want to do that. Well, actually I *did* want to complain, but I wouldn't let myself.

"You know what I've been thinking?'' Stephanie said.

"What?'' Kate asked, reaching for the bread basket.

"Well, since our parents are going to be buying our artwork anyway, why don't we make our own art gallery?'' Stephanie said. She took the bread basket from Kate and ripped off a couple of pieces.

"The Sleepover Friends Gallery. I like that!'' Kate said. "Where would we have it, though?''

"How about out in my apartment?'' Stephanie suggested. She was talking about the playhouse her parents built for her in their backyard. Ever since the twins were born, we've had most of our sleepovers out there. It has matching fold-out couches, a sink, a counter with stools where we can eat, and even a mini-refrigerator. It's even decorated in Stephanie's favorite colors: red, black, and white.

"We should also have a trophy case for the blue ribbons we're going to win — all four of them!" Kate agreed.

Patti said, "It's a good thing none of us is interested in doing something in the same category — giving out ribbons makes the art fair pretty competitive."

I'd been thinking the exact same thing. Doing an art project was bad enough. Having it judged was the worst!

"Maybe we should all keep our projects a secret," Stephanie suggested. "It'll be more fun that way. Then we can surprise each other at the art fair."

I set down my fork and sighed. I hadn't meant to sigh so loudly. It just sort of came out.

"What's wrong, Lauren?" Patti asked.

"Well, first of all, it's going to be easy keeping my project a secret from you guys because I haven't decided on a category, much less a specific project," I said.

"How about drawing?" Kate suggested. "Everyone can draw."

"I can't," I said. I couldn't help thinking Kate should know that, too. "Remember when Ms. Gilberto had us draw those animals?"

Stephanie nodded. "Hope drew a great family of mice."

"Well, I drew Rocky . . . and he came out looking like a walrus," I told them. And Rocky is my *cat!*

"Lauren's right. Drawing is out. Get your list of categories, Patti," Kate commanded in her take-charge voice. "We're going to decide right now what Lauren should do." Kate pulled her glasses out of her pocket, a sure sign she was ready to get serious. "It'll have to be a category that one of us isn't already doing something in, of course. But that shouldn't be hard, since there were so many to choose from."

Patti knit her eyebrows. "I don't think Lauren's project should be a group decision — she should decide for herself. Lauren's the one who has to do it."

I knew Patti was right. But part of me wanted to just let Kate take over. I was trying to decide which way to go, when Stephanie broke the silence.

"You know what would really help Lauren — and the rest of us, too?" Stephanie said thoughtfully. Then, answering herself, she said, "A theme. That way, even though our projects will be really different, they'll be connected. It will make our Sleepover Friends Gallery even better, too."

18

It was Kate's turn to scowl. "Theme? Like what?" Kate's quick to give ideas, but she isn't always so quick to accept other people's.

Stephanie grinned. "The perfect theme, of course. Friendship — as in the four Sleepover Friends."

"I like it," Patti said, and even *I* had to smile.

"Friendship it is," Kate said.

We were finished eating, so we started to clean the kitchen and load the dishwasher.

"I wonder what Hope's weaving looks like?" Stephanie mused, as she wiped the table.

"Me, too," Kate agreed. "You know, we should really invite her to a sleepover."

"How about the next one?" Patti suggested.

"Our next sleepover is at my house," I said.

"Perfect," Stephanie said. "Hope will love your house, Lauren." My family recently moved to a big, old house that I called "Nightmare Mansion" at first. But now I like it a lot.

"What's for dessert?" I asked Kate.

"Spumoni ice cream," Kate said with a flourish. She'd managed to keep it a secret all day. But then Kate doesn't have trouble *keeping* secrets, it's having secrets *kept* from her that drives her wild.

"And don't forget my mother's peanut-butter-chocolate-chip cookies," Stephanie added.

"I've got a great idea," Patti said. "Why don't

19

we all go to the Riverhurst Art Museum tomorrow? It's bound to be inspiring."

"I have to baby-sit for the twins in the afternoon, but I could go in the morning," Stephanie said.

"I know I can go," Kate said.

"My dad's going to his office on campus tomorrow morning," Patti said. "I bet he'd be glad to drop us off. How about it, Lauren? Can you go?"

I took a quick bite of cookie. I wasn't that excited about spending Saturday morning at an art museum. But then again, looking around might help me get my brain working. I was about to say that I'd go when I felt sharp pain in one of my teeth.

"Yeow!" I cried.

"What's wrong?" Patti asked.

"My tooth," I said. I rubbed my jaw and looked at the cookie I was holding. "Maybe there was something in this cookie."

Stephanie took the cookie from me. Since her mother had made them, she looked kind of insulted. She examined it and handed it back.

"Nothing in there but chocolate chips and a few walnuts," she said.

"It must have been a walnut or a chocolate chip." I put the cookie down.

"Biting a walnut shouldn't hurt that much. Maybe you have a cavity," Kate suggested. "You should probably see a dentist, just to make sure."

I sighed. "I already have an appointment with Dr. Nadler for next week."

Patti looked at me sympathetically. "I know how you feel, Lauren. I saw Dr. Nadler a little while ago, and he thinks I might need braces." Patti peered at my mouth. "Do you think you might need braces, too?"

"I don't think so. This is just my regular checkup," I said. Then I rubbed my cheek. "I hope I don't have a cavity, though." Somehow, a cavity sounded even worse to me than braces. I'd never had one before, and I didn't want one now.

"How about the art museum tomorrow, Lauren. Can you go?" Stephanie asked.

For once I was glad Stephanie had changed the subject back to art.

"Sure," I said.

"Great! We're all going then," Kate said.

"What should we do now?" Patti asked after we'd finished cleaning up the kitchen. "I got some new Mad Libs yesterday. We could do those."

"How about listening to dedications on WRBM?" Stephanie suggested. WRBM is a local station that takes dedications on Friday night. It's mostly high-school kids dedicating songs to their boyfriends or girlfriends. It's fun for us to try to guess who they're talking about. Like when they say RH, they might mean my brother, Roger Hunter.

"That sounds good to me," I said. I'm pretty good at guessing whose initials are whose because I know lots of Roger's friends.

"There's a great movie on 'Friday Night Chillers' tonight," Kate put in. "It's called *Haunted Hands,* and it's about this artist who loses his hands in an accident. The doctors sew his hands back on, but they accidentally sew on the hands of a *criminal* instead. The artist wants to draw and create like usual, but his hands just want to strangle people and steal things."

Patti laughed. "And it even has an art theme."

We took the cookies and Kate's spumoni ice cream and headed upstairs to watch "Friday Night Chillers."

Art theme or not, the movie was pretty awful. I hate scary movies, anyway. As I watched it, I kept thinking, *I* have hands like that. Not criminal, of course, but definitely out of control. I wanted my hands to create something fantastic for the art fair, but I was sure they were going to do exactly what they'd always done . . . create an art disaster.

Chapter
3

"What should we look at first?" Kate asked when we arrived at the museum Saturday morning.

"How about checking out the folk art exhibit?" Patti suggested. Kate nodded, and we started walking toward the wide marble stairs leading to the second floor.

"It's too bad Hope isn't here," Stephanie said as we rounded the corner. I knew what she meant. There were all sorts of woven hangings along one wall that Hope probably would have loved.

We looked at the wall hangings for a while. Or rather, Stephanie, Patti, and Kate did. I glanced at them, but I didn't think they were all that interesting. So I headed over to the water fountain down the hall.

And it was a good thing I did. Because if I hadn't, I never would have seen a roomful of cat art! It was right around the corner from the wall hangings.

There were paintings of cats and drawings of cats. But, best of all, there were several sculptures of cats! Unlike the drawings and paintings, the sculptures looked solid and lifelike. I wanted to reach out and stroke one that looked like my own cat, Rocky. I didn't, of course, because there were signs all over the place saying DO NOT TOUCH.

All at once I had an idea so brilliant it surprised me. I would make a clay sculpture of a cat for the art fair! None of the Sleepover Friends was doing a sculpture. And it would fit in with the Sleepover Friends theme, too. After all, my Rocky was the brother of Stephanie's cat Cinders, Patti's cat Adelaide, and Kate's cat Frederika. It was absolutely perfect! I would call it "Sleepover Cats Forever!"

By early that afternoon, I began to realize my idea wasn't going to be as easy as I'd thought. I was trying for the tenth time to draw a picture of what I wanted my sculpture to look like, when the telephone rang. It was Kate.

If we were still neighbors, Kate would have just come over instead of calling. But our new house is way out on Brio Drive. That's a long way from my old house, and Kate's house, on Pine Street. We were still within biking distance of each other, but you definitely called before you came.

"How's it going?" Kate asked. I knew she was

dying to find out exactly what I was doing, but I wasn't about to tell her.

"A little slower than I'd hoped," I said casually. "How about your project? Are you getting a lot done?"

Kate sighed. "Yes and no. I'm definitely doing photography, but it isn't easy trying to figure out the best way to approach our theme."

I shook my head. It was hard to listen to Kate complain about what seemed like a minor problem to me. She'd probably be tearing her hair out if she had the kind of problems I was having!

"At least tell me what category you decided on," Kate wheedled.

"Oh, all right. I'm doing a sculpture," I admitted.

"Lauren! That's great! Of what?" Kate asked.

"Oh, no you don't, Kate Beekman! It's supposed to be a surprise, remember?" I reminded her.

"Oh, all right," Kate sighed.

I laughed. But I wasn't fooled for a minute. I knew she was going to keep trying to get it out of me.

"Want to meet at the mall tomorrow?" Kate asked. "We can buy our supplies and hang out."

"This isn't another trick to try to find out the details of my project, is it?" I asked suspiciously.

"On my honor," Kate promised innocently. "I

guess I'll just have to wait and find out at the art fair like everyone else."

"Okay, then. What time?" I asked.

"How about noon? That's right when the mall opens on Sunday," Kate said.

"Sounds good to me," I said. "I'll call Stephanie and Patti and see if they can meet us, too."

When I reached the entrance to the mall on Sunday, I saw that Kate's bike was already there. Patti's was next to Kate's on one side, and Stephanie's fifteen-speed was on the other side. I locked my bike and hurried in to find them.

"There you are, Lauren," Kate said when I joined up with them outside Hale's Hobby and Craft Shop.

I looked at my wristwatch. It was only ten after twelve.

"I just got here, too," Stephanie assured me.

"Well, what is everyone going to buy?" Kate asked. She was looking right at me and rubbing her hands together.

"I need to buy clay," I said. I'd decided that doing a drawing of my project first was useless since I couldn't draw. I was going to buy some clay and charge right ahead.

"Lauren's doing a sculpture," Kate told Patti and Stephanie.

"All right!" Patti cheered. "I knew you would come up with a good idea, Lauren. Were you inspired by what you saw at the art museum yesterday?"

I smiled mysteriously. "As a matter of fact, I was."

"Maybe it wasn't such a good idea to keep our project a secret from each other," Kate mused. I smirked. Then we all went into the store.

Hale's Hobby and Craft Shop had everything from knitting needles to silk watercolor paper.

Stephanie went over to look at fabric paint, and Kate headed straight for the photography section.

It took Patti and me a little longer, but we finally found the clay — a whole aisle of it. Some was gray, some was red, and some was white. Some was wrapped in plastic and some was in buckets. There were about a million different kinds in all. It was bewildering.

"I'm getting a headache," I told Patti as I looked over the choices.

Patti nodded. "I know what you mean. It *is* a little overwhelming."

I picked up the nearest package. The clay was a dark red color. "Do you think I can paint this clay after it dries?"

"I don't know," Patti admitted. "Maybe we should ask someone."

"Ask someone what?" a familiar voice asked. It was Jenny Carlin — and her sidekick, Angela Kemp.

I quickly stuck the package of clay behind my back. I didn't want Jenny or Angela to know what I was planning. I couldn't afford to have the fragile buds of self-confidence I was nurturing trampled by an insensitive oaf like Jenny.

"Oh, nothing," I said, trying to sound casual.

"Hi, Jenny. Hi, Angela," Patti said. Patti is nice to practically everyone.

"I suppose you two are here for the same reason we are," Jenny said. She was peering at me, trying to see what I had hidden behind my back.

Carefully, I set the clay back on the shelf behind me. Then I let my hands drop to my sides.

"I suppose," I said. "Come on, Patti. Let's go." Patti gave me a funny look, but she didn't argue.

"Bye," I said as Patti and I began backing away.

"Toodles," Jenny called after us. I shuddered. She has the most irritating voice in all of Riverhurst.

"I thought you were going to buy that clay for your sculpture," Patti said once we'd gone around the corner and Jenny and Angela were out of sight.

"I was. But I didn't want those two to know. I'll get it after they leave," I said.

We found both Kate and Stephanie up front by the cash register. It looked like Kate had just bought

28

half the photography supplies in the store, but Stephanie hadn't bought anything.

"I'm really excited about my photography," said Kate as we headed out into the mall. "Especially since I'm going to do all the developing work myself. Dad knows someone at the hospital who has a darkroom I can use." Kate's father is a doctor at Riverhurst Memorial.

"All this art has made me hungry," I told them. "Let's grab a slice of pizza at the Pizza Palace."

"Sounds good," Patti said.

I told Kate, Stephanie, and Patti to keep an eye out for Jenny and Angela, and snuck back to the clay aisle. The coast was clear. I grabbed the first package I could find, ran back, paid for it, and we were on our way to the Pizza Palace.

The Pizza Palace isn't really a palace. In fact, it's closer to a closet than a palace. There's just a little kitchen in the back and a counter with stools, a few round tables, and four video games out front. But John, the owner, makes great pizza and sells it by the slice.

Usually, the place is packed. But I guess early Sunday afternoon is John's slow time, because it was empty when we walked in.

"It smells so good in here," Kate said. I agreed wholeheartedly.

A few minutes later, the four of us were sitting at the counter in the Pizza Palace waiting for our order: four slices of meatball pizza and four cherry colas.

"You'll never guess who Patti and I saw in Hale's," I said. I pulled a straw out of the dispenser and started peeling off the paper.

"Jenny Carlin and Angela Kemp," Kate said.

"You saw them, too?"

"No," Kate said. "But I'm seeing them now."

I spun around just in time to see Jenny and Angela come strolling in.

"Oh, no," Stephanie groaned.

Patti waved at them and said, "Hi, again."

"Oh, hi," Jenny said as if she had just noticed the four of us sitting at the counter. "Having pizza?"

It was a totally dumb question. There's nothing else to have at the Pizza Palace. But Patti nodded and said, "Yep." Sometimes she's *too* nice.

"What's in there?" Kate asked Jenny. Kate nodded at the big bag Jenny was holding. It had HALE'S printed across it in big black letters.

Jenny smirked. "That's for me to know and you to find out." Then she turned to Angela. "I've changed my mind about pizza. Let's get something else."

Angela mumbled something I couldn't hear. Then they turned and walked out.

"Well, excuse me," Kate said, imitating Jenny's whiny voice.

I laughed. "You're excused," I said.

"Here's your pizza, ladies," John said. He put a paper plate with a steaming slice of meatball pizza in front of each of us.

"Ambrosia," I declared. I opened my mouth to take that first fabulous bite. But, as I bit down, I had another sharp pain in one of my back teeth.

"Ouch!" I cried, dropping the pizza back on the plate.

"Too hot?" Patti asked.

I shook my head.

"Is something wrong with the pizza?" John asked.

"There's something wrong with Lauren's tooth," Kate said. "Isn't there, Lauren?"

I nodded. Once might have been an accident. But having a pain twice like that in less than twenty-four hours was definitely not a coincidence. I was sure now that Kate was right. There *was* something wrong with one of my teeth!

I sadly watched Patti, Kate, and Stephanie enjoy their pizza, but I wasn't going to take any more chances with mine.

I tried to comfort myself by remembering that I was scheduled to see Dr. Nadler on Wednesday. I liked Dr. Nadler. He would fix things up for me.

Meanwhile, I'd work on my project and try to forget about my teeth.

When I got home, I rushed right up to my room and unwrapped the clay. I was eager to get going. I knew what I wanted my sculpture to look like — now if I could only get the clay to cooperate.

At first the clay was hard. I squeezed it for a while. Then it became soft and gooey. It smelled weird. It also turned my hands red. I struggled to turn the red mudlike stuff into a sculpture of my cat.

I tried to make a sculpture of Rocky sitting upright. I gave him a long, graceful neck. But when I added the head, it made the neck slowly bow until my sculpture looked more like a wilted flower than a cat.

I looked over at Rocky, who was curled into a ball sleeping peacefully on my pillow. I decided to do a sculpture of him like that. Then my sculpture just looked more like an oval lump of mud!

"Lauren!" It was my mother. "Dinner!"

"Coming," I called back. I looked down at my hands. There was nearly as much clay on them as there was on my sculpture.

I left the ball of clay sitting on the newspapers on my desk and went into the bathroom to wash. Before long, the sink looked as awful as my hands — which still weren't clean.

"Lauren!" This time it was my father calling me.

"I'll be right there!" I called back. I lathered up my hands and rinsed them one more time. But it was no use. My hands looked just like the hands in that horror movie *Haunted Hands*!

"Lauren Hunter!" It was my father again.

I looked at the dirty sink. It would have to wait until after dinner. I quickly wiped my hands on the nearest towel, which left more red stains. The towel would have to wait until later, too.

"Where have you been?" Mom asked when I came into the kitchen. We were having hamburgers, one of my favorites.

"Washing my hands," I said, slipping into my chair.

Mom looked down at my red hands. "You washed them? What did they look like before?"

"Worse," I assured her.

"What have you been doing, anyway?" Dad asked.

"Art," I told him. I picked up my hamburger and took a big bite. The first bite tasted good. That is, until my tooth started giving me trouble.

"What's wrong?" Mom asked when I grimaced.

"I've got this pain in my mouth," I admitted. I opened my mouth and pointed toward the back. "White ere," I said. I meant right here, of course.

"You'd better go to the dentist," Dad said.

"She's going on Wednesday," Mom said. "Don't forget now, Lauren."

"I won't," I promised.

"It's all that junk you eat," Roger said, shaking his head. "You know, Lauren, stuff like those barbecue potato chips aren't just bad for your *teeth*. Natural athletes like you and me need foods that build our bodies, not rot them."

"Roger has a point," Mom said.

I felt like they were ganging up on me. But I did like having Roger call me a natural athlete.

"I don't eat all that much junk," I said. But even as I said it I knew it wasn't true. I *did* eat a lot of junk food, and, from the looks of things, I was going to have to start thinking about cutting back.

I was too upset about my teeth to do any more work on my project that night. Instead, I took a long hot bath and went to bed.

Chapter
4

"Oh, no!" I cried. It was Monday morning, and the first thing I saw when I opened my eyes was red clay. My whole supply had dried out overnight because I'd forgotten to put it back in its plastic bag. Now it was lying in a crusty-looking heap on the newspapers I'd spread out to protect my desk.

"What's wrong?" Mom asked, sticking her head into my room.

"My project is ruined before it even got started," I told her.

Mom came in and looked at the mess on my desk. "What was it before?" she asked cautiously.

"A ball of clay," I admitted. "I was sort of between things. I should have put it back in the plastic bag before I went to sleep. Now it's dried out."

"Looks like all you need is more clay," Mom said in her most reasonable tone of voice.

"I need more than just new clay, Mom. I need creativity," I told her.

"You're very creative," Mom insisted. Of course, I didn't believe her. Mothers have to say things like that, even when they're not true.

"I'm glad you think so," I said.

Mom patted my arm. "Cheer up, Lauren. Roger said something about going to the mall after school today," Mom said. "I'm sure he'll be glad to take you with him so you can pick up some more clay. Get dressed now and come downstairs. I've made French toast for breakfast."

I put on jeans and a blue pullover sweater. As usual, my hair was limp and as straight as a stick. I brushed it, but that didn't help. Finally, I gave up trying to look nicer than I felt and went down to the kitchen.

Mom put a plate of French toast in front of me. "Eat this. It'll make you feel better."

Roger popped in the back door a few minutes later. "Have we got a date this afternoon, Squirt?" he asked.

"I guess," I said gloomily.

"Something wrong?"

I shrugged and said the only word I could think of. "Art."

Roger laughed and said, "I get it. The suffering artist, right? Well, see you after school."

36

School wasn't as bad as I had thought it was going to be. We played a great game of softball at recess. Pete Stone was one of the team captains and chose me first for his team. That made me feel good. I actually hit a homer and helped make two double plays, too.

When I got home that afternoon, Roger was there waiting for me. "Let's move," he said. Then he smiled. "If we get back here fast enough, I'll go jogging with you."

"All right!" I cried. I love jogging with Roger. He makes me run really hard, but afterward I always feel great.

"I'll meet you out here in twenty minutes," Roger said as soon as we were inside the Riverhurst Mall.

"Okay," I told him.

As I walked toward Hale's, I saw Alan Reese and Kyle Hubbard from 5A leaving the store with big bags of stuff.

"Hi, Lauren," they said when they saw me.

I waved and hurried into Hale's.

I had just picked up another bag of red clay when I spotted Jenny Carlin. Again! There was no place to hide, and anyway, I still had to pay for my clay. So I held my ground, waiting for her to see me and say something snide.

But Jenny didn't seem to notice me, even though

she was just a few feet away. She looked pretty frazzled, and her hands and fingernails were a deep shade of red. It dawned on me Jenny had been making something with the very same clay I'd been using! She picked up another bag of the cursed red clay. For a moment I held my breath, but then Jenny looked right at me.

At first, she just blinked her eyes really fast. Then her gaze dropped to the bag of clay *I* was holding. Before I could think of something to say, Jenny flung her bag of red clay into her shopping cart. Then, without even bothering to say hello to me, she hurried toward the front of the store.

I wanted to scream. It was bad enough being an art klutz without having Jenny Carlin trying to show me up. Knowing Jenny, she was probably even doing a sculpture of a *cat*!

For a second I considered giving up. But I couldn't do that, either. I'd let Patti, Kate, and Stephanie down if I gave up, not to mention Mrs. Mead, Ms. Gilberto, and all the sick kids at the new children's hospital. I groaned. Fifth grade was so complicated.

By the next morning, I couldn't wait to get out of the house. I wanted to be as far away as possible from my clay mess.

I'd been so eager to get back to my project after

38

my run-in with Jenny Carlin that I'd even given up jogging with Roger. I'd moved my work to the basement, and spread newspapers all over Mom's laundry table. Then I'd dumped the lump out and began squeezing it.

After a while, I'd made something that actually looked a little like a cat. It also looked a little like a *dog,* and a little like a *bear,* and even a little like a *pig.* I'd really tried to convince myself it was good enough. Of course, it wasn't. But by then, it was dinnertime, and I still had homework to do, so I'd put the cat-dog-bear-pig back into the plastic bag.

"How's it going?" Kate asked as I slid into my desk that morning. "Have you made any progress on your sculpture?"

"It could be going better," I admitted, after checking to make sure Jenny Carlin wasn't within earshot.

"The clay isn't working out?" Kate asked.

"Not yet," I said. I showed Kate my hands. "Maybe you could just take a picture of these for me. There's probably just as much clay on my hands as there is on my sculpture." I'd probably *still* have red hands and gross nails when I was in college.

Kate shook her head. "You know what your hands remind me of?"

"Don't say it," I warned as I quickly stuck my hands out of sight under my desk. I knew she was

39

going to say the artist in *Haunted Hands*.

"Maybe I could help you," Kate suggested. "I don't really know all that much about — "

"Shhh!" I said, cutting her off.

Jenny Carlin and Angela Kemp had just walked into the classroom.

"Jenny's trying to copy my project," I whispered to Kate once they'd walked past us. "I don't want her to know about all the trouble I'm having."

"She's copying *you*?" Kate asked. "Why would she do that?"

"My guess is she's trying to make me look bad," I said. "She wants to humiliate me by outdoing me."

Kate was about to say something else, but the bell rang. Mrs. Mead stood up and started class. Soon we were doing fractions. After that we had a spelling test. Thankfully, there was no talk about art or art projects again until Mrs. Mead dismissed us for lunch.

Once we were sitting down at our regular table, though, Kate told Stephanie and Patti what I'd told her that morning about Jenny.

"How can you be sure that's what she's doing, Lauren?" Patti asked.

I told Patti about my run-in with Jenny in Hale's.

"Well, I wouldn't worry about it if I were you, Lauren," Patti advised. "Jenny isn't particularly good

40

in art. She certainly isn't better than any of the rest of us."

"Patti's right, Lauren," Kate agreed. "Whatever you do will be a hundred times better than whatever Jenny does."

I thought of my cracked clay ball. Then I thought about my cat-dog-bear-pig. "I wish I were as sure about that as you all are."

"You just have to get acquainted with your medium," Kate assured me.

"I guess so," I said.

"Besides, you aren't the only one who's being copied," Stephanie said. She quickly looked from side to side. Then she motioned for the rest of us to move in a little closer. "It's about Ginger and Christy."

Ginger Kinkaid and Christy Soames are in 5C. I had liked Ginger Kinkaid when she first moved to Riverhurst. But Ginger is the kind of girl who can only have one best friend at a time. When she realized I had three best friends and wasn't going to give them up to be just *her* best friend, she dropped me — fast. Now her best friend is Christy Soames. Christy's okay by herself — but when the two of them are together, they're awful.

When we were close enough, Stephanie whispered, "I think Christy Soames and Ginger Kinkaid stole my fashion design sketches!"

"Really?" Kate gasped. Stealing was serious business.

"I brought them to school yesterday morning," Stephanie said, "but when I was getting ready to go home yesterday afternoon, they were missing. *Then,* this morning I saw Christy and Ginger huddled over some *drawings.* When they saw me looking in their direction, Christy scooped everything up. It was obvious she didn't want me to see whatever it was!"

"Did they look like your sketches?" Patti asked. "Maybe you just misplaced them."

But Stephanie shook her head. "I saw Christy and Ginger out by the water fountain later. This time, they didn't notice me."

"Did they have your sketches?" I asked.

"No. But they were arguing about Christian LaPerle!" Stephanie exclaimed.

"What's Christian LaPerle?" I asked. It sounded like a toothpaste.

Stephanie scowled at me. "Not *what* — *who.*" Then she got a dreamy look on her face. "He's only the most fabulous fashion designer of the decade. Devi Glinton, Laura Dallas, and Michael Geo are just a few of the big rock stars who wear Christian LaPerle creations."

"Oh," I said. I happen to think Devi Glinton looks like she picked out her clothes while blindfolded, but I didn't say anything. Stephanie knows a lot more about both fashion and rock music than I do.

But, of course, Kate spoke right up. "You mean someone actually *designs* clothes for Devi Glinton?" she said. "She actually spends *money* on those rags she wears?"

Stephanie frowned. "Well, a lot of people think Christian LaPerle is hot, Kate. Anyway, Ginger and Christy must think so because they've stolen my sketches."

"Are Christy and Ginger working together?" I asked. That possibility had never crossed my mind. "I mean, I didn't know you could work with another person like that."

Stephanie shrugged. "Most people aren't, but those two are. They're partners in crime. And I'm going to find out what they're hiding!"

"You mean, spy on them?" Kate asked.

"Uh-huh. Why not?" Stephanie said enticingly.

"Because it isn't right," Patti said.

"Was it right of them to steal my sketches?" Stephanie demanded.

"Two wrongs don't make a right," Patti said staunchly. "Besides, just look over there." Patti nodded her head at a table on the other side of the lunch room. We were too far away from Christy and Ginger to hear what they were saying, but it was obvious that they were arguing about something.

43

"Maybe they're having an attack of guilty conscience," Patti suggested.

"Hmm. Maybe," Kate said. She gave her Jell-O a thoughtful poke with her fork, sending it into a spasm.

"Well, I want those sketches back," Stephanie declared.

"I think if you just wait it out, Stephanie, they'll bring them back," Patti said. "That is, if they really did take them. Maybe you just misplaced them or something."

Stephanie didn't look like she believed Patti, but before she could say anything else, Hope Lenski came over to our table.

"Hi," Hope said, sitting down.

"Hi, Hope," Kate said. "We've been wanting to ask you something. We're having a sleepover at Lauren's this Friday. Can you come, too?"

"Really?" Hope looked pleased. "I'd like to, but I'll have to check with my dad first. Okay?"

"That's fine," I said. "I hope you can make it."

Chapter
5

"How have your teeth been, Lauren?" Dr. Nadler asked me Wednesday afternoon. I'd ridden my bike to his office right after school. Now I was sitting back in his chair with my feet up.

I looked at Dr. Nadler's drill, which was right in front of me. I wanted to lie and say, "Just fine!" But, of course, I couldn't. "Pretty good," I mumbled instead.

Dr. Nadler lifted one big bushy eyebrow and said, "*Pretty* good, huh? What's wrong?"

"I guess one of my teeth has been bothering me," I confessed.

Dr. Nadler interrupted before I could say any more. "Do you eat many sweets?"

"Well, some," I said guiltily.

He shook his head. "You may have to start watching what you eat."

I felt my cheeks turn red. Of course Dr. Nadler was right. There was Kate's marshmallow fudge, the Dr Peppers, the chips, the dips, the cookies. . . . It made me hungry just thinking about it!

Dr. Nadler said, "Well, Lauren, open up and we'll take a look."

After he poked around in my mouth for a while with his metal pick, Dr. Nadler took some X rays. Then he polished my teeth.

"Do you think I have a cavity?" I asked when he was all through. I looked at that drill again and shuddered.

"I'll know for sure in a little bit," Dr. Nadler said. "Why don't you go out to the waiting room for just a minute?"

"Okay," I said, even though I really didn't want to. After a few minutes, Mrs. Kluez, Dr. Nadler's receptionist, motioned to me to come over. "Your X rays are developed," she said. I braced myself for bad news. "You'll need to schedule another appointment with Dr. Nadler."

"You mean I have a cavity?" I said. I felt like crying.

"You have three," Mrs. Kluez said matter-of-factly as she got out Dr. Nadler's appointment book. I suppose you get hardened after working around cavities day in and day out.

"Three!" I cried. I'd never thought beyond the possibility of *one*! Three cavities!

"Yes, but Dr. Nadler feels he can take care of all three of them in a single appointment. How would next Tuesday be for you? You could come to the office right from school again," Mrs. Kluez suggested brightly.

The room seemed to fill up with fog. My forehead felt damp and my palms got all sweaty. Even my vision blurred. That horrible drill in Dr. Nadler's office was going to be drilling *my* teeth!

"Okay," I said weakly. My throat was too tight to say anything else.

"Very good," Mrs. Kluez said pleasantly. "We'll see you then."

I just stood there for several seconds. Then I walked outside in a daze and got on my bike. I barely remember riding home. When I got there, I sank into the nearest chair. I felt really sorry for myself. It seemed to me I didn't eat more junk than my friends. Why was I the only one to get cavities?

Just then Mom got home. Great.

"Lauren!" she exclaimed cheerfully. "How did it go at the dentist, sweetie?"

I looked up sadly. Both Mom and Dad had been proud of my perfect dental checkups. I didn't know how they'd react to this.

"Lauren," Mom said again. "How did it go?" She walked across the room and stood in front of my chair. I didn't want to tell her, but I knew I had to.

"I have three cavities," I mumbled.

"What?" she said, even though I'm sure she heard me the first time.

"I have three cavities," I said again, a little more loudly.

"*Three?* That's a lot." She shook her head.

"I know," I said. "It's awful. I have to get them filled next Tuesday."

"What's awful?" Roger asked, coming through the kitchen door.

"Lauren has *three* cavities," Mom said. She sounded pretty upset.

"Like I told you, Lauren, you're going to have to cut down on the junk food," Roger said, shaking his head. He held up the apple he was munching. "This is the kind of snack you should eat."

"Roger is right," Mom said in her no-nonsense voice. "I think you're going to have to take a serious look at your eating habits." Then she turned around and headed upstairs.

Slowly I got up and went to my room. I had a lot to do — two pages of math homework and a short story to read. Then, of course, there was my dreaded art project. I wasn't in the mood to face any of it. Instead, I just sat on my bed, brooding about how

48

unfair life could be. Then Rocky strolled into the room.

When he saw me sitting there, he stopped for a minute and said, "Meow?" Then, without waiting for an invitation, he jumped into my lap.

Naturally, I began petting him. Soon he rolled onto his back and started purring. Just having him there making that nice noise made me feel a lot better. It seemed like a sign, too. I had to forget about my teeth for the moment and get on with my art project, which was, of course, my clay sculpture of a cat.

"You're cute," I told him as I scratched under his chin. He looked up at me adoringly. "But you're going to have to get down now. If I'm going to immortalize you in clay, I have to get going."

I picked Rocky up and set him gently on the floor. Then I trudged downstairs and got to work. But my burst of energy only lasted about half an hour, or until my father got home.

"Lauren!" I heard him call down the basement stairs. "I want to talk to you."

"Just a minute, Dad," I called back. I was squeezing what had been my cat-dog-bear-pig back into a shapeless blob.

"Right now!" Usually my dad has a pretty good sense of humor, but I guess his sense of humor doesn't extend to cavities.

49

I looked at my clay. After all my work, I was back to square one. I rinsed off my hands as best I could — at least I was getting better at that — and ran upstairs. It was Dad's turn to give me a dental lecture.

"So, how was the dentist?" Kate asked when I met up with her, Patti, and Stephanie at the bike rack before school on Thursday.

"Horrible," I said. "I have three cavities. My parents are furious. Even Roger started lecturing me about eating habits."

"That's too bad," Patti said sympathetically.

"They're threatening to put me on a guinea pig diet — strictly fruits and raw vegetables," I said glumly.

"Is that so bad?" Patti asked. She pulled open the heavy side door and held it while we all went into the school.

"Yes! If I eat like a rodent, I'll probably end up looking like a rodent." I thought longingly of all my favorite foods (now all forbidden) and sighed.

We'd almost reached Mrs. Mead's room when I stopped suddenly. "Look over there," I whispered.

Christy and Ginger were standing in front of their classroom, 5C, but they were too involved in whatever they were doing to notice us. Ginger was holding a rumpled bag.

50

"Do you think Christy and Ginger have your sketches in that bag, Stephanie?" Kate asked in a hoarse whisper.

Stephanie's face turned pink. "Ah . . . no," she said hesitantly.

"I bet they do!" I said. "Look how they're hovering over it."

Stephanie pulled a folder out of her notebook. "They don't have my sketches because my sketches are right here," she said sheepishly.

"What?" Kate asked.

"They gave them back?" I guessed.

"Actually, I found them. They were at home, under my bed the whole time," Stephanie admitted.

"Well, I'm glad we never said anything to Christy and Ginger about stealing," Patti said pointedly. "That would have been really embarrassing."

"They are stealing my idea, though," Stephanie grumbled. "I just know whatever they're doing has something to do with Christian LaPerle."

"Hi." Hope came up behind us. "Is this a meeting of some kind?"

Kate laughed. "No, not really."

"Well, I talked to my dad," Hope said, "and I can come to the sleepover tomorrow night. What should I bring? Something to snack on?"

"Lauren's giving up junk food," Kate said. "So don't bring anything to tempt her."

"Not by choice," I assured Hope. "I have three cavities."

"Too bad," Hope said sympathetically.

"We're all trying to cut back on junk food," Patti said firmly. Kate's eyebrows went up.

"Good idea," Hope said. "Too much sugar isn't good for you."

"Then it's settled," Patti vowed. "We'll all eat healthfully from now on." She looked right at Stephanie and Kate, who had been exchanging alarmed looks.

"I guess it wouldn't hurt. . . ." Kate said reluctantly.

"Well, if everyone else is going to, I guess I will, too," Stephanie relented.

"I'll bring some zucchini bread with me Friday night," Hope volunteered. "It has a touch of brown sugar in it, but it's really good for you otherwise."

Stephanie looked stricken. "Vegetable *bread*?" she said. "Is it green?"

Hope laughed. "Sort of, I guess. It tastes like cake, though. I'm sure you'll like it, Stephanie."

Zucchini bread? I thought to myself. Yuck! Give me marshmallow fudge and barbecue potato chips any day! I didn't say what I was thinking, though. After all, they were doing this for *me*.

* * *

When I got home from school that afternoon, I resigned myself to tackling my art project first thing. But when I went downstairs, I couldn't find my clay anywhere.

"Were you still using that?" my mother asked when I called her at work to ask about it.

"It was my art project," I said.

"Oh, Lauren! I'm terribly sorry. It was garbage day today, and I was doing a quick check of the house this morning," Mom explained. "When I saw that bag lying on my laundry table, I just assumed it was something you'd meant to throw away. I should have asked, but I was in a hurry."

"Don't worry, Mom," I said. "I can get some more." After all, there was a ton of the stuff at Hale's.

As soon as I hung up, I got my bike and took off for the mall. Replenishing my clay supply was becoming second nature. I had almost reached the bike rack when I saw Mrs. Green's station wagon stop by the mall entrance, and Stephanie climbed out.

"Stephanie!" I called, speeding up.

Stephanie stopped and turned around. "Hi! What are you doing here?" she asked.

"What else? Getting more clay. My mom accidentally threw out what I had," I explained, getting off my bike and locking it. "What are you doing here?"

"I'm going to check out the fabric store. I'm not sure they have the right material here in Riverhurst. I might have to go to the city this weekend if they don't," Stephanie explained.

I was impressed. Stephanie really sounded like she knew what she was doing.

"I'll go to the fabric store with you if you'll come to the hobby shop with me," I offered.

"Sure," Stephanie said. "Then we can go to Sweet Stuff. My treat."

My hand flew up to my cheek. "I'll go to Sweet Stuff with you," I told Stephanie as we walked along, "but I'm not eating anything from there."

"Sorry, Lauren," Stephanie said. "I forgot about your cavities."

"I wish I could forget about them," I said glumly.

Suddenly, Stephanie grabbed the sleeve of my jacket and pulled me into the nearest store, Creative Costumery.

"Hey," I said, "what's going on?"

"I just saw Ginger and Christy. I think they're going into Material Pleasures," Stephanie said excitedly. Material Pleasures is the name of the fabric store. "I don't think they saw us."

"So what if they did?" I asked. There was a weird display of rubber alien masks on the wall next to us.

It was giving me the creeps. I wanted to get out of there.

"Let's follow them," Stephanie said. "I want to see what they're going to buy."

"Sure. Why not?" I said. Kate and I used to spy on Roger all the time. It had been fun.

Stephanie stuck her head out the door of Creative Costumery and peered down the mall. "They're gone," she said. "They must have gone into Material Pleasures, just like I thought." Stephanie slowly edged out of the store and slunk down the mall toward the fabric store. I followed her.

The front of Material Pleasures is all glass — which means it's hard to sneak up to the entrance without being seen. But the inside of the store is cluttered with bolts of fabric in long rows — with plenty of places to hide.

"Okay," Stephanie said. "If they do see us, act like we're just in here looking around. We don't want them to know that we're spying on them."

I nodded. "Gotcha."

We slipped inside and I instantly spotted Ginger's hair. It's hard *not* to notice her hair — it's reddish-brown and long, thick, and wavy. I'd give anything to have hair like that.

"There she is," I whispered to Stephanie. Stephanie nodded, then crept slowly from one bolt of fabric to the next, getting closer and closer to where Ginger and Christy were in the next aisle. I followed her.

We were almost there when I heard Christy say, "This is perfect!"

"I don't know," Ginger said. "I like this one better."

"Are you kidding?" Christy demanded. "No way!"

Ginger sighed. "We've got to decide, Christy. We're running out of time."

"Maybe we should each do our own separate project after all," Christy said. "It would be a lot easier." She sounded really fed up.

"But not as much fun. Let's do this," Ginger said. I knew Ginger well enough to know she was getting ready to suggest a compromise that would eventually let her have her own way. "Let's get a sample of each and take them home with us. This stuff can look different in different lighting."

"Okay," Christy agreed reluctantly. "But we've got to decide by tomorrow. We've still got a lot of work to do."

"Uh-oh," Stephanie hissed. "Here they come!"

Stephanie backed up quickly, so quickly that she backed into me before I could move out of the way. I lost my balance and fell backwards, pulling a couple of bolts of fabric with me! Stephanie fell, too — right on top of me! I couldn't help giggling. We must have looked pretty ridiculous. Stephanie said, "Shhh!" But

Christy and Ginger walked down the other aisle without even hearing us.

After they were past, Stephanie stood up. Then she helped me to my feet.

"Sorry, Lauren," she apologized, but she was giggling, too.

"That's okay. Did you see the material they were arguing about?" I asked.

Stephanie shook her head. "No," she said sadly. "And I can't buy anything myself until I *do* know, either. This," she said fiercely, "is war!"

"Forget it, Stephanie," I said. "Their project is going to be a disaster. Those two aren't going to agree on anything."

"But that's the Christian LaPerle look," Stephanie said sadly. "They're going to outdo me for sure!"

When we got to Hale's Hobby and Craft Shop, I noticed a display case along the back of the store that I hadn't seen on Saturday. In the case were a few of the models that Hale's sells. There were also a couple of paintings. But what interested me the most was a little statue of an elephant. "Plaster Sculpture," it said on a little piece of paper.

"Isn't that great?" I asked Stephanie.

She nodded. "It looks like marble, doesn't it?"

I decided then and there to forget the clay. I'd use plaster. The shiny, marblelike surface would make my cat sculpture look almost regal, I told myself. But, best of all, the stuff was *white*. It wouldn't look nearly as gross under my fingernails!

I also found a book called *Sculpting with Plaster* that explained how to do it. Then I found the kind of plaster the book suggested using.

As I was paying for my stuff, I thought I saw Jenny Carlin out of the corner of my eye. I turned around quickly, but no one was there after all. Stephanie hadn't seen her either. I decided that I'd been imagining things.

"Stress," Stephanie said, and I believed her.

Chapter 6

"Should I use just one picture?" Kate asked as we sat down for lunch on Friday. "Or should I use four pictures, you know, one for each of us?"

Kate was still having trouble deciding exactly what represented the Sleepover Friends' friendship in the best way. Meanwhile, I was still wishing I had Kate's problem instead of my own. We'd been working on our projects for the art fair for a whole week already, and I didn't have anything to show for it except a couple of chapped hands.

So far, plaster wasn't working any better for me than clay had. When I'd gotten home from the mall Thursday afternoon, I'd rushed right down to the basement, eager to make my new, plaster cat sculpture.

But right away, I'd had trouble mixing the plaster. First it was too watery. Then it was too lumpy.

Finally, I got a nice block of the stuff to actually harden. But when I'd tried to carve it like it showed in the book (which had cost me a small fortune), the plaster crumbled into a fine, white powder.

By then, it was after six and I'd decided to call it a night. I also decided to call my latest venture "Lauren's Plaster Disaster." I couldn't help wondering if *anyone* would be willing to bid on a plastic bag of plaster dust. Not even my own parents would go for it. I shook my head sadly and looked at my lunch.

Kate tapped her finger thoughtfully on her chin. "Or maybe I should use a picture of something symbolic, like a bird in flight. What do you guys think?"

But before Patti, Stephanie, or I could say anything, Pete Stone, at the table next to ours, said, "Maybe it should be a picture of a *balloon,* showing what an airhead you are, Beekman!"

"Wise guy!" Kate replied. She wadded up her napkin and tossed it at him. Pete ducked, and it hit Kyle Hubbard instead.

"Hey, Beekman," Kyle said. "Get a coach! Your aim is terrible." He was just kidding, of course. Kyle and Kate had been in the same class the year before, and are actually pretty good friends. Kate probably would have laughed if Jenny Carlin hadn't started snickering. She was sitting at a table on the other side of us with — you guessed it — Angela Kemp.

Naturally, Angela started snickering, too. It was a duet of snickering.

"Quit snickering, Carlin," Kate said, turning the other way and glaring at Jenny and Angela. "I don't know what you have to laugh about anyway. How's *your* art project coming?" Kate demanded pointedly.

"Fabulously," Jenny said with a superior air. She glanced at me for a second and snickered again.

"Fabulously," Mark Freedman, who was sitting with Kyle and Pete, mimicked Jenny. The boys guffawed and poked each other with their elbows.

"Go ahead and laugh," Jenny said. Her face was turning red. "But I'm going to win first place in the sculpture division at the art fair. We'll see who laughs then."

"Oh, really?" Stephanie said. "With your *clay* sculpture?" Stephanie looked at me and winked. She was the only one of the Sleepover Friends who knew I'd switched from clay to plaster.

"No," Jenny said. "With my *plaster* sculpture."

"Plaster!" I was outraged. "When did you switch to plaster, Jenny Carlin?"

"None of your business, Lauren Hunter." With that, Jenny stood up. "Come on, Angela. Let's go. I've had enough lunch."

I was outraged. "She switched to plaster because *I* switched to plaster," I whispered so the boys wouldn't hear.

61

"When did you switch to plaster?" Patti asked.

"Lauren changed her mind yesterday afternoon," Stephanie explained. Then, turning to me, she said, "I guess that *was* Jenny you saw in Hale's yesterday, after all, Lauren."

I shook my head. "What am I going to do now? I can't even mix up the plaster the right way."

"Just do the best you can," Patti said sympathetically.

"I've got a better idea. We'll help you at least get the stuff mixed up right," Kate promised. "Our sleepover's at your house tonight anyway, Lauren. Right?"

I sighed. "I was hoping we'd do other things at the sleepover, like have fun."

"Maybe you're right," Kate agreed. "Well, *I* could come over right after school," she offered.

"Really? That would be great," I said. If anyone could whip that plaster into shape, it was Kate!

"I have to watch the twins for a while before I come to the sleepover," Stephanie said. "Otherwise I'd help, too."

"And I've got to stay with Horace until Mom and Dad get home from their monthly history department meeting at the university," Patti said.

"That's okay. Kate and I will manage," I said.

* * *

62

"I don't know much about plaster," Kate warned when we were at the bike rack unlocking our bikes after school. "But it shouldn't be hard to figure out."

Little did Kate Beekman know how hard a simple thing like mixing up plaster really was. I knew, because I'd tried it already. But maybe with Kate helping me, things would be different.

Kate and I used to ride our bikes to school together a lot back when we were neighbors. So it seemed like old times as we rode off together that afternoon.

When we turned the first corner, I was surprised to see Hope riding her bike a little ways ahead of us. Hope lives near me, but she doesn't usually ride her bike. Her father drops her and her brother Rain off in the mornings, and then picks them up again in the afternoons. Hope's mother stayed in California after her parents' divorce so she isn't around at all. According to Hope, Dr. Lenski grew up in Riverhurst, and that's why he decided to move back here.

"Hope, wait up!" Kate called. Hope stopped riding and turned around. When she saw us, she waved.

"Where are you guys going?" she asked when we'd caught up with her.

"I'm going to Lauren's to work on Lauren's art project," Kate said.

"You're doing a sculpture, aren't you, Lauren?" Hope asked.

"I'm still *trying* to do a sculpture," I said. "So far, it's been a losing battle. It's plaster, six, and me, zero."

Hope laughed, then said, "The important thing about plaster is to get it mixed just right."

I rolled my eyes. "Tell me about it. So far, I haven't been able to get past that."

"Want me to come over and help?" Hope offered. "I've mixed plaster before for Dad, you know, for casts for animals with broken limbs."

"Really? Then you know what you're doing! That would be great!" I said.

"I'll just stop off at home and make sure it's okay," Hope said. "I'll be over in ten minutes or so. Okay?"

"More than okay! Thanks a lot, Hope," I said.

When we reached Hope's corner, she turned. "See ya' in ten," she called over her shoulder. Then she raced off on her mountain bike.

Kate and I got to my house and leaned our bikes against the front steps. Then I unlocked the door and we went in. "Let's have a snack," I said, heading for the kitchen. "I'm starved."

"So what else is new?" Kate asked.

"What's new is that I'm eating healthy snacks now. No more junk food," I reminded Kate.

Kate shook her head. "I suppose that means I have to.eat healthy, too."

"If you want," I said. "I'm having an apple. But there's plenty of other stuff around here still." I pulled open the cupboard next to the sink. "See? Chips, cookies, crackers — "

Kate shook her head. "Close that cupboard!" she declared. "If you can eat healthy, so can I."

I tossed Kate an apple. "That's the spirit," I said. "Let's take these apples downstairs and get started."

"Do you think we should wait for Hope?" I asked when I was showing Kate all my past disasters. I gave the bag a little kick, which sent a puff of plaster dust into the air. "It sounds like she knows her way around plaster."

Kate knelt down by the bag and brushed off the mixing instructions. "Well, if it turns out that she can't come, we'll have wasted valuable time by waiting. And these directions don't sound too hard to follow," Kate said as she looked them over. When she was finished reading the directions, Kate said, "I see what your problem has been."

"You do?" I said, peering over her shoulder. Leave it to Kate, I thought happily to myself.

"Well, sure. It says here that you need a helper to stir while you add the water. You've been trying to both stir and add water, haven't you?" she said.

I shrugged. "I really haven't had much choice."

Kate smiled up at me. "There, you see? Everything's going to go really smoothly now that I'm here," she told me confidently. She picked up the mixing bucket, carried it over to the laundry tub, and turned on the water. I brought over the bag of plaster, then we began to mix.

"Don't stir too vigorously or bubbles will form," Kate quoted from the directions. "Squeeze out those lumps," she ordered. "Don't splash!" she cried.

I was starting to get a little annoyed. "I've done this before, you know," I told her.

"I'm just repeating the directions," she said. "Anyway, you said it didn't work before."

"It didn't," I admitted.

Suddenly, there was a loud crash right over our heads!

"What was that!" Kate said. There was a second loud crash, followed by a strange scuffling noise.

Kate and I looked at each other. Then, at the same time, we both cried, "Bullwinkle!"

I dropped the stirring stick I'd been holding, and Kate dropped the measuring cup. Then we dashed up the basement stairs.

"Oh, no!" I cried when I saw the kitchen floor. There were big muddy paw prints everywhere. It *was* Bullwinkle.

"He's supposed to be in the backyard," I told Kate.

"Obviously, he isn't," said Kate.

"Obviously," I agreed. "But how did he get in the house?"

Then I saw Hope. She was standing just inside the door.

"I let him in," she said in a small voice.

"Oh," I said.

"I knocked a bunch of times," Hope explained, her words rushing out. "I figured you were probably in the basement and didn't hear me. The door was unlocked, so I thought I'd just come in since you were expecting me. But as soon as I opened the door, that giant black dog just *shot* in. I tried to stop him, but he must have seen the cat."

"Rocky!" Kate and I cried at the same time. Then all three of us dashed out of the kitchen. The living room looked worse than the kitchen had! Two lamps had been knocked over, and there was broken glass all around one of them. There was a muddy paw print on the seat of Dad's favorite chair, and Mom's ivy was lying in a pile of its own dirt. But there was no sign of either Rocky or Bullwinkle.

Then I saw the paw prints on the stairs. "Upstairs!" I cried, moving fast. We had to contain this disaster before it got any worse! Hope and Kate followed me.

We found them in my room. Rocky was on top of my bookcase. His back was arched and he was hissing at Bullwinkle. Bullwinkle was drooling and wagging his tail. His attention was focused entirely on Rocky, so he didn't notice us sneaking up behind him.

"Gotcha!" I cried as I threw my arms around his enormous black, furry neck. Bullwinkle reared, and Kate grabbed his collar.

"I'll get the cat," Hope said confidently. But as soon as she reached for Rocky, he leaped away from her. Then he jumped down from the bookcase and dashed toward the open bedroom door. Bullwinkle lunged as Rocky shot past him, and I lost my grip on Bullwinkle's neck. At the same time, Kate let go of Bullwinkle's collar.

"They got away!" I said as the two animals escaped into the hall.

"Oh, no!" Hope wailed. "Look what they've done to your room, Lauren!"

I looked around my room. Actually, it looked pretty much the way I'd left it that morning.

Kate laughed. "Lauren's room always looks like this," she told Hope.

Hope looked embarrassed. "Oh," she said. "Never mind."

"Let's go! We've got to get Bullwinkle back outside where he belongs before anything else gets broken," I said, heading for the bedroom door.

"Right!" Kate and Hope agreed.

By the time we finally wrestled Bullwinkle outside again, Roger came home.

"What happened?" he asked, surveying the damage.

"Bullwinkle and Rocky strike again," I told him.

"It's my fault," Hope said. "I let Bullwinkle in."

"It was an accident," I said.

"We'd better get this mess cleaned up before Mom and Dad get home," Roger said. "I'll get the bucket and sponge mop from the basement."

Kate and I looked at each other. "The plaster!" we cried. All four of us ran to the basement. Sure enough, the plaster we'd been mixing was too hard to stir anymore.

"You'll have to get it out, Lauren. We need that bucket to clean the floors upstairs," Roger said.

"Well, here goes nothing," I said. I turned the bucket upside down and tapped on the bottom. Nothing happened so I tapped a little harder.

"Here, let me," Roger said. He took the bucket and gave the bottom a good whack! with his fist. The plaster fell out and broke into four jagged pieces as it hit the floor.

"Oh, no," I cried. "Now I have to start all over again!"

"Wait, Lauren! Not so fast!" Kate said. "I think you've got something there."

"What I have here is another mess," I said forlornly.

Roger took the bucket and headed for the stairs. "I'm going to mop up the mud."

"We'll be up in a minute to help," I told him. Kate picked up one of the pieces of plaster and set it on the workbench.

"What does this look like to you, Hope?" Kate asked.

Hope shrugged. "A hunk of plaster?"

I giggled. "It looks like a bag of french fries to me."

Kate grinned. "It does to me, too." She picked up a second piece of plaster. "If you sanded down the edges of this, you'd have a hamburger."

"That does look a little like a hamburger!" I exclaimed.

"And this piece could easily be an apple, and that one an orange." Kate arranged the four chunks side by side. "There you have it!"

"Have what?" I asked.

"Your sculpture for the charity art fair," Kate said. "The war between the healthy and the unhealthy food!"

"Is a hamburger unhealthy?" I asked.

"Of course a hamburger is unhealthy!" Hope exclaimed. I wasn't so sure a nonvegetarian would agree with her.

"I don't know," I said. "I was going to do a sculpture of a cat." The secret was out, but it didn't matter at this point.

"You could sand these pieces and mount them on wood. You could even paint them," said Kate. "And it all fits in with our theme, too."

"What theme?" asked Hope.

"The theme of the Sleepover Friends' friendship," I explained.

Kate nodded. "All the Sleepover Friends are going to be cutting back on junk food so Lauren won't have to do it alone, you know, like we talked about at lunch yesterday." She held up her apple core to prove her point. "It's a war, because each of us, especially Lauren, really likes junk food."

"Oh, I see, I guess," Hope said. But she didn't really look convinced. I wasn't sure either, but I was getting pretty desperate. I was ready to go along with just about anything.

Chapter
7

"Kate and Stephanie are here, Lauren," my mother called up the stairs at seven o'clock that night.

"Send them up, please," I called back.

I was in my room cleaning up. After the fiasco with Bullwinkle and Rocky that afternoon, I'd decided my room could use a little help.

Now I looked around quickly. My sweaters weren't in the corner anymore. I'd just stuffed them in my chest of drawers, but at least they were out of sight. There was nothing on my floor anymore except my blue rug. I'd even put clean sheets on my double bed and straightened up the junk on my desk. Kate would probably still think my room was messy. But then everyone's room is messy next to Kate's. I did want Hope to notice the difference, though.

Kate came in first. "Hi, Lauren." She set her

overnight bag neatly at the foot of my bed. "*The Curse of the Mummy's Crypt* is on 'Friday Night Chillers' tonight." That sounded safer than the one we'd watched at Patti's.

"We've only seen *that* one three times, Kate Beekman," Stephanie said, coming in right after Kate. "I, for one, refuse to watch it again!" Stephanie tossed her stuff onto the bed.

"I've got a much better idea." Stephanie pulled out my desk chair and sat down. "We can take this quiz in *Teen Topics* as soon as Hope and Patti get here."

"What kind of quiz?" I asked. But before Stephanie could answer, the doorbell rang again.

"That's probably Patti," Kate said.

"Or Hope," Stephanie said without looking up from her magazine.

"Last I heard, Patti's dad was going to pick up Hope on the way over here," I said. "It's probably both of them."

"Hi," Hope and Patti said as they came into my room together. Hope was looking around my room. She looked amazed and I felt kind of offended. It was cleaner, but not *that* much cleaner.

"I picked up a little," I confessed.

"This is a great room, Lauren. It's so big," Hope said. She came in and sat down on the floor with her stuff. "Before I forget," she said, unzipping her bag and taking out a foil package, "here's the zucchini bread I said I'd bring."

"Great! That will fit right in with the rest of tonight's healthy menu," I said.

Stephanie eyed the package warily. "What does that mean, Lauren?"

"It means we're going to eat healthy snacks tonight, like we agreed," I said. "Let's go down and load up before we start taking that quiz of yours, Stephanie. I'm starving. Besides, there's something I want you all to see."

"I brought a plate of my fudge," Kate said. "I gave it to your mother, Lauren. She said she'd put it in the kitchen."

"Uh-oh," Patti said as we left my room. "I don't think marshmallow fudge qualifies as a healthy snack, Kate."

"It qualifies as a *fantastic* snack, though," Stephanie said.

I shivered as I remembered the pain I'd felt in my cavity. Kate's fudge was definitely on the "forbidden" list. "Maybe so," I said, leading the way down the stairs. "But I'll have to pass it up, at least until I get my mouth repaired. I don't think I can give up Kate's fudge forever, though."

"The key is moderation," Patti said.

I opened the kitchen door and sighed. Moderation had never been one of my strong points, especially when food was involved. But I was determined to turn over a new leaf.

"Get a plate for this zucchini bread, will you, Kate?" I said.

Kate got a plate and I unwrapped the bread.

"It looks good," Patti said kindly. But, I noted, it *was* pale green, just as Hope had said it would be.

"Uh, it does look good," Stephanie said doubtfully.

Hope picked up a knife and cut off a slice. "Try it, Lauren."

"Okay," I said. I gingerly bit off a corner. I was surprised. It *was* good! I smiled and took a bigger bite. "This tastes like spice cake."

Hope smiled triumphantly. "I knew you'd like it. You're next, Stephanie." She cut off another piece.

I popped the rest of my piece into my mouth. "Look, while you all sample Hope's zucchini bread, I'm going to run downstairs and get something."

"I think I know what it is," Kate said. "Do you need any help bringing it up, Lauren?"

"Not really. I want all four of you to see this at the same time," I said.

I flicked on the basement light and hurried down to get the plaster pieces. I'd been giving it a lot of thought. If Patti and Stephanie could see the same things that Kate had seen, I was going to go ahead and finish the "Junk Food versus Healthy Food" sculpture.

When I got back up to the kitchen, I laid the plaster pieces out on the kitchen counter. "Well," I said, "what do you think?"

Patti looked down at the four pieces and frowned. "Is that what you did after school?" she asked cautiously.

"It was sort of an accident, but it's — " I began to explain.

"Wait!" Stephanie cried, interrupting me. "Let me guess. It's sports equipment, right?"

I looked at the pieces again. The piece that Kate said could be an orange *did* look a little like a basketball, now that Stephanie mentioned it. My mind raced. Should I call the plaster fragments "Sleepover Friends Sports Equipment" instead of "Junk Food versus Healthy Food"? But what kind of sports equipment did Stephanie think the bag of fries was — home plate after a slider? Besides, Kate hates sports, and Stephanie's not exactly a jock either. Sports equipment just didn't fit our theme.

"Well, no," I finally said. "It's not sports equipment. I guess it could be, but it's not."

"It's healthy food versus junk food," Kate said impatiently. "Anyone can see that. I think it's great."

"What's that piece again, Lauren?" Hope asked. She was pointing at the hamburger.

"A hamburger?" I said.

"Is the hamburger healthy food or junk food?" Patti asked.

I looked at Hope, expecting her to answer for me. Just then, the back door burst open, and Roger *and* Bullwinkle came in.

"Oh, no!" I said. "Quick! Someone grab the rest of the zucchini bread!" We never leave any food lying on the counter when Bullwinkle is in the room.

Patti snatched up the plate. But Bullwinkle ignored Patti and lunged in my direction.

"Arggh!" I cried. I closed my eyes and braced myself for the big, wet, Bullwinkle kiss I was sure was coming.

But when nothing happened, I opened my eyes. Instead of putting his huge black paws on me, Bullwinkle had put them up on the kitchen counter, and he was about to chow down on the plaster hamburger!

"Oh, no!" I cried as I saw his teeth sink into the white plaster. I closed my eyes again. It was too horrible to watch.

There was a strange noise, sort of a series of crashes.

"Is it . . . you know?" I asked, my eyes still closed.

"I'm afraid so, Lauren," Kate said sadly. "It's back to the bucket for you."

77

I opened my eyes to see for myself. Bullwinkle had white powder all around his mouth. There was a puzzled look on his face.

"What was that?" Roger asked. He grabbed Bullwinkle and pried his mouth open.

"My sculpture for the art fair," I said sadly, as Roger pulled a few mangled chunks of plaster out of Bullwinkle's mouth. The rest of my sculpture was all over the kitchen floor. It hadn't been the best piece of art in the world. It hadn't been the best piece of art I'd ever made. It hadn't even been what I'd really wanted to make, either. What it had been was *finished,* and that had been enough for me.

"I'm really sorry, Lauren," Roger said. He frowned at Bullwinkle, who didn't look the least bit sorry. In fact, if Roger hadn't been holding him by the collar, Bullwinkle might have tried to eat up the plaster fragments as well. To each his own, I guess.

"I didn't know you guys were in here or I would have left Bullwinkle up in my apartment." Roger's room is above our garage — he calls it his apartment.

I glanced at Kate, expecting her to look mad. After all, it was her idea that Bullwinkle had just demolished. But instead of looking mad, Kate actually looked pleased. "See," she said triumphantly. "*Bullwinkle* knew that was a hamburger, even if the rest of you didn't."

78

Even I had to laugh at that. Stephanie, Patti, Hope, and Roger laughed, too. I think even Bullwinkle was smiling. It's hard to tell with Bullwinkle, though. He mostly smiles with his eyes.

"I'll get the broom," Kate said.

"I'll get Bullwinkle out of here," Roger volunteered.

Roger and Bullwinkle went out the back door again. Kate swept up. Patti, Stephanie, and Hope helped me get out the snacks. There were rice cakes with peanut butter, pretzels (low-sodium), apples and oranges, popcorn (air-popped with no caramel), and sugar-free chocolate pudding. I'd even gotten my mother to pick up sugar-free Dr Pepper for us.

"Sugar-free Dr Pepper?" Kate muttered when she saw it. "Somehow it just doesn't seem right."

We loaded all the food into the dumbwaiter, then went upstairs to haul it up.

"This dumbwaiter is fantastic," Hope said as I pulled up our load.

We carried the stuff into my room. Everyone got settled. Patti handed out the cans of sugar-free Dr Pepper. Kate picked up a rice cake and examined it like it was something from a science experiment gone wrong.

"Are you sure this is eatable?" Kate asked suspiciously.

"It's a rice cake, Kate," Hope said, taking one

herself. She bit into it. "Mmm. These are great. One of my favorite snacks."

Kate shrugged and bit into the one she'd taken. She made a funny face. Then she set the rest of the rice cake down and picked up her sugar-free Dr Pepper. After taking a big drink, she said, "I'm sorry, Hope. That thing tastes like a Styrofoam cup."

Hope giggled. "I guess it does taste a little like that, now that you mention it. Not that I've ever eaten a cup."

"Okay," Stephanie said. "Settle down, everyone. We're going to take this quiz now."

"What is it, anyway?" I asked.

I picked up a rice cake and took a bite. I thought it tasted all right. If anything, it tasted like *nothing*. If it hadn't been for the peanut butter, I would have forgotten I was eating anything.

"It's called Doodle Analysis. It tests your creativity quotient," Stephanie said. She reached for some pretzels.

"Oh, no," I groaned. "Anything but that!"

"How about *The Curse of the Mummy's Crypt*, then?" Kate asked hopefully.

"No," Stephanie said firmly.

Patti suggested a game of Truth or Dare.

"What's that?" Hope asked. I couldn't *believe* she'd never played it before!

We explained that you either had to answer a

really horrible, personal, question, or do something outrageously embarrassing.

Hope said, "I think I understand. I'll go first." Hope really was a good sport.

"Okay, Hope," I said, "truth or dare?"

Hope thought for a minute, then said, "Truth."

"Did you think those plaster fragments really looked like junk food versus healthy food?" I asked mercilessly.

"Lauren!" Hope cried. "That isn't fair."

"You picked truth," I reminded her.

"Well, I'm not exactly into abstract art," Hope said tactfully.

"That wasn't my question," I said. I wasn't going to let her off the hook. There's no room for tact in Truth or Dare.

"All right. The truth, then." Hope sighed. "I think Bullwinkle was probably an art critic in one of his past lives."

Even I had to laugh at that. "It was awful, wasn't it?" I said.

"I think you can do something better," Patti offered.

"I want to go next," Stephanie said. Then, without waiting for Hope to say truth or dare, Stephanie said, "I'll take dare. I want Hope to dare me to go over to Ginger's and spy on Ginger and Christy. I really want to see what their project looks like, and

I know they're both over at the Kinkaids' this very minute working on it!''

"You know that's not how Truth or Dare works,'' Kate said. "You can't tell Hope what the dare should be.''

"Why not?'' said Stephanie stubbornly. "We can all sneak over to the Kinkaids'. It's nice out tonight, and it would be fun.''

"It's too late to go that far away,'' Patti pointed out.

"Patti's right,'' I said. "My parents would have a fit if they found out we were wandering around Riverhurst in the dark.''

"Besides, didn't we agree that spying on them would be wrong?'' Patti asked.

"You and Hope agreed,'' Stephanie said to Patti, "but I never did. Lauren never did either.''

Kate grinned wickedly. "I think spying is fun. It's pretty harmless, too.''

"Unless you're the one being spied on,'' Patti said, folding her arms across her chest.

"According to the rules of the game, I get to decide the dare, don't I?'' Hope said, bringing us back to the real issue. We all nodded — even Stephanie.

"Well, then, I *dare* you to wait until the art fair to see what Ginger and Christy's project is,'' Hope said with a mischievous glint in her eye.

Patti smiled. "I think you're a natural at this game, Hope."

Hope returned Patti's smile. "Thank you, Patti."

Stephanie shook her head. "That's one of the hardest dares I've ever been given. But, I accept."

"I'm next," I said. "And I want Stephanie to dare me to spy on Jenny Carlin. I'd like to see just how Jenny's making out with *her* plaster project. Maybe we could even bring Bullwinkle with us," I added, wiggling my eyebrows suggestively. I didn't know if Bullwinkle was up for a second plaster snack in one evening, but it was certainly worth a try.

"Lauren!" Kate cried. "You are truly awful!" She said it like a compliment, though.

"Thanks," I said.

Chapter
8

Saturday morning, Dad made pancakes for everyone. He said the pancakes were our reward for being so quiet during our sleepover. He really appreciated not having to get up several times to tell us to settle down like he usually does. He was also glad we hadn't tried to sneak outside.

I'm sure Hope was wondering what our sleepovers were usually like. After all, we'd stayed up really late. We'd eaten everything in sight. We'd even telephoned a couple of boys — I'd dared Patti to call Henry Larkin and ask him how his art project was going. Patti had turned a dark shade of red while she talked to Henry. That's probably because we were all gathered around her, listening. Somehow, though, she managed to sound perfectly normal. It was a riot.

Then Kate had dared Stephanie to call Taylor

Sprouse, the sixth-grader she thinks is so incredibly cool. Kate told Stephanie to ask Taylor where he got the new black jacket he'd been wearing all week. But Taylor knew right away who Stephanie was from the sound of her voice, and hung up on her before she got to ask her question. Stephanie was outraged! That was a riot, too.

Luckily, Dad missed all that. His pancakes were great, even if he did make us eat them with apple-sauce instead of syrup.

"I've got to go," Stephanie said as we carried our plates to the sink. "Mom promised to help me with my art project this morning while Dad watches the twins."

Kate and Patti said they needed to go home to work on their projects, too.

"How about you, Hope?" I asked, when she didn't say anything. "Have you got plans?"

Hope yawned. "I sure do. I plan to go back to bed as soon as I get home. I just hope I don't fall asleep while I'm riding my bike."

"It takes a while to get used to missing so much sleep every Friday night," Patti told Hope. "It took me at least two months."

"Really?" Kate said. "Two months?"

Patti nodded. "I bet all that time you guys thought I was really shy. But I wasn't — I was just tired!" We all laughed.

After everyone left, I cleaned up the kitchen until it sparkled. Loading the dishwasher, sweeping up crumbs, and even wiping off the counter tops seemed like more fun than going downstairs and mixing up another batch of plaster!

Finally there was nothing left to do, so I sighed and started down the basement stairs.

The open bag was waiting for me right where I'd left it. I got out the mixing bucket and a pitcher full of water. I read the directions again. Then I pushed up the sleeves of my oldest rag of a sweatshirt and got to work.

What seemed like hours or possibly even days later, I was trying to make myself believe that the blob of plaster in front of me looked like a cat, when I heard the basement door open.

"Are you down there, Lauren?" It was Roger.

"Yes," I said with a sigh.

"Can I come down?" Roger said. "Bullwinkle isn't with me."

"Maybe you *should* get Bullwinkle," I said. "He seems to know how to deal with bad art." I looked at my pathetic sculpture. Why, I asked myself, had I ever decided to do a sculpture in the first place? Roger pounded down the stairs in his size-thirteen sneakers. "Does this look anything like a cat to you?" I asked him, indicating the mound of plaster in front of me.

"Well . . ." he said hesitantly.

"Don't lie," I warned him. "I'm not in the mood for lies."

"It *does* look more like cat *food* than a cat," Roger admitted. "Say, you know what all this plaster reminds me of?" he asked. "That time I fell off the Freelanders' garage and broke my arm. You know, that gives me an idea. Have you ever heard of a sculptor named George Segal?"

"No, I don't think so. Is he famous?" I said.

"Pretty famous. He actually puts plaster casts on people, all over them, front and back. Then he takes the hardened plaster off them and puts it back together to make a life-size statue. It's really something. I bet you could do something like that, too, Lauren," Roger said thoughtfully. "It doesn't look like it would be very hard."

It did sound interesting, and I was desperate enough to consider just about anything. "Have you got something I could look at?" I asked. "You know, something that shows what this guy's finished pieces look like?"

"I don't," Roger said. "But I bet the library does. Get your jacket. I'll drive you over there and help you look. It's the least I can do."

Dad dropped me off at school Monday morning because I'd overslept and missed my bus. It had been a long weekend.

First I'd read from cover to cover the book on George Segal's art I'd gotten at the library. His art was really interesting, and Roger had been right. It didn't seem all that hard to do. There had even been a chapter in the book called "Notes on Technique." I read that chapter twice.

Sunday afternoon I made a quick trip to the drugstore. I had plenty of plaster, but according to the book, I needed petroleum jelly, too. If I didn't use that, the plaster would stick to my model and hurt when I took it off again. I didn't want *that* to happen, especially since *I* was going to be the model!

By the time I got home, I remembered that I still had homework to do. I stayed up until almost ten finishing that. I never did get to work on my new, revised, art project. No wonder I overslept!

"Don't forget to put the meatloaf in the oven at four-thirty," Dad said as he pulled to a stop in front of Riverhurst Elementary.

"I won't," I said. I thanked Dad for the ride and hurried into school. I couldn't wait to find Kate, Stephanie, and Patti and tell them what I'd seen at the drugstore on Sunday.

Everyone, including Hope, was in the hall outside our classroom when I walked up.

"Hi," I said, joining them. "I overslept this morning. Dad had to drive me here or I would have been late."

"It's that new diet, Lauren," Stephanie said. "Eating only healthy foods is making you weak."

I laughed. "Actually, staying up until ten o'clock getting my homework done made me weak," I said. I was actually doing all right on my rodent diet. It was boring, but at least my cavities weren't hurting all the time. "I got so involved in my art project this weekend, I forgot all about my other homework."

"I spent a lot of time working on my project, too," Patti said. "It's gotten so interesting that I lost all track of time." She yawned. "Mom had to tell me to go to bed three times last night before I finally went."

Then Hope, Patti, Kate, and Stephanie all started talking at once, about how interesting their projects were. That didn't surprise me. They had all been excited about the art fair from the beginning. What surprised me was that I was finally just as excited as they were. In fact, I was so interested in my new idea that I could hardly wait to go home to work on it some more!

"You're still using plaster for your sculpture, aren't you, Lauren?" Stephanie asked.

I nodded. "Roger gave me a great idea. I can't wait to show you guys at the art fair — that is, if I can pull it off."

"You will," Patti said.

"Meanwhile, I'm sure this will cheer you up, Lauren," Stephanie said. She paused for a moment and looked around. Everyone else had gone into class because it was almost time for the bell to ring.

"I guess it's safe," Stephanie said. "When I was at Hale's yesterday buying some fabric paint, I happened to see Jenny Carlin." Stephanie grinned wickedly, her dark eyes twinkling.

"Has she given up on plaster?" I asked hopefully. Finding out something like that would really make my day.

Stephanie shook her head. "She sure looked like she wished she could, though. Jenny was buying *three* more bags of the stuff!"

"Wow!" Kate said. "Maybe her sculpture is going to be humongous!"

I nodded. "Either that, or she's having major problems!" I giggled.

"Well, when I asked her what she was going to do with all of it," Stephanie went on, "she glared at me and said, 'None of your beeswax!' "

Kate chuckled. "Beeswax! That sounds just like Jenny, all right. Dumb."

Patti said, "She must be having as much trouble as you were, Lauren."

I shrugged. "Maybe." But I couldn't help being a little worried. What *was* Jenny doing? I was going

90

to go crazy wondering if her project was better than mine!

"You're not the only one who saw someone buying supplies this weekend, Stephanie," Kate said. "I saw Jane Sykes buying watercolors at the mall on Saturday. She looked pretty embarrassed when she saw me. Remember? She was telling everyone on Friday that she'd finished her art project. I think she's just starting it."

"Or starting it over," I said, thinking about myself. "Are you guys finished with your projects?" I asked. I was a little worried. The art fair was this coming Saturday — there were only five days left until then.

"I'm close to being done," Kate said. She looked pleased.

"Me, too. It's taken a while, but I'm finally on the right track," Patti said.

Stephanie smiled mysteriously. "I'm not giving out *any* details about my project. The walls have ears around here."

"How about you, Hope?" Kate asked. "How is your weaving coming along?"

"Slowly, but I really like the way it's turning out," Hope said. "Do you all want to come over to my house after school tomorrow and see the loom? My dad said that would be a good day for him."

91

Patti, Kate, and Stephanie all said they'd like to, and I was about to say I would, too. Then I remembered that I had my appointment with Dr. Nadler on Tuesday, right after school.

"I can't," I said, leaning back against the lockers. "Tomorrow's D-day. That's D as in *dentist*."

"Ugh! Getting cavities filled isn't fun," Kate said.

"Poor Lauren," Patti said sympathetically, just as Jenny Carlin and Angela Kemp walked up.

"What's wrong, Lauren?" Jenny asked in that horrible, whiny voice of hers. "Having trouble with your art project?" She sounded so hopeful that for a second I saw red.

"No, but I hear you — " I began, intending to say something about Jenny's three bags of plaster. But Patti nudged me with her elbow.

So I simply said, "No," instead. But I couldn't stop myself from adding, "Are you?"

Jenny smiled smugly. "As a matter of fact, I *was* having a little trouble. But now I think everything is going to be just fine."

"We'd better go into class now, Jenny," Angela said. "The bell is about to ring."

I looked at the hall clock. For once, Angela was right. We followed them into Mrs. Mead's class, and just barely made it into our seats in time.

"Today I'm going to hand out the admission

tickets for the art fair, class," Mrs. Mead said as soon as everyone was quiet. She held up a big roll of tickets. "As I said before, I hope everyone will sell at least fifteen tickets. Are there any questions before I hand them out?"

Naturally, Karla Stamos's hand shot up. Mrs. Mead called on her.

"I'd like more than fifteen," she said smugly.

"That's wonderful, Karla. In fact, anyone who is sure they can sell more than fifteen, raise your hand. I might as well give them to you right away," Mrs. Mead said.

Jenny Carlin raised her hand. "I think I can sell a hundred tickets," she said.

"A hundred?" Mrs. Mead raised her eyebrows.

"She means her father can sell a hundred tickets," Henry Larkin whispered loudly. Mr. Carlin is a big shot in Riverhurst.

Jenny spun around and gave Henry a withering look. He just grinned. I could see why Patti likes him so much.

"Well, I'm sure the people at the children's hospital don't care who sells the tickets. The important thing is raising as much money as we can for such a worthy cause," Mrs. Mead said.

Karla looked really burned up. There was no way she could sell a hundred tickets herself. I could see that Karla thought her goal of becoming teacher's pet had just moved out of her reach.

Mrs. Mead counted out Jenny's hundred tickets first. Then she went over to Karla's desk. "How many extra tickets did you want then, Karla?" Mrs. Mead asked.

"I'll just take fifteen," Karla mumbled.

Mrs. Mead didn't say anything. She counted out fifteen tickets and handed them to Karla.

"I bet my dad could sell a few extras at the hospital," Kate whispered. "What do you think, Lauren?"

"Sure, why not?" I whispered back. I wasn't going to take any extras, though. I still had my art project to do, and time was rapidly running out.

Chapter
9

"Good luck, Lauren," Patti said at the bike rack after school Tuesday.

"Thanks," I said. I needed all the good luck I could get. Not only was I about to go to Dr. Nadler's to get my teeth filled, but I had discovered that making a plaster cast of my arm wasn't as easy as I thought it was going to be. In fact, my wonderful new plan had turned out to be another plaster disaster. I also had my art fair tickets to sell. My parents had bought two, and Roger had bought two. That left eleven more to go.

"I wish you were coming to Hope's house with us, Lauren," Kate said.

"I do, too," I said.

"Why don't you come over after you get finished at the dentist's?" Hope suggested. "My dad won't be

95

taking everyone home until five-thirty or so. That's when he closes his clinic."

"Maybe I will," I told her. Hope's house is just around the corner from mine. It would be a quick bike ride.

"You probably won't feel like it," Stephanie predicted. "I know I didn't feel like doing anything after I got my tooth filled. And I only had one cavity. You have *three*."

"Thanks for reminding me, Stephanie," I said. "I might have forgotten."

"Sorry," Stephanie apologized, pulling up the collar of her red-and-black jacket and pretending to hide behind it.

"Well, if you *do* feel like it, come," Hope said as we all took off on our bikes. I rode with them for a few blocks, then turned toward Dr. Nadler's office.

I parked my bike in front of the big wooden door that said DENTIST. Then, with a sigh, I pulled open the door and walked in.

I felt my throat tighten up with fear, and I couldn't help thinking about Bullwinkle and the way he whines whenever we pull up in front of the vet's with him. I wanted to whine, too. But, of course, I couldn't.

"Lauren," Mrs. Kluez said when she saw me, "you're right on time, dear. Go on in. The doctor is waiting for you."

I gulped. She sounded like someone in one of those horror movies.

"These are all just little surface cavities," Dr. Nadler said as he put cotton in my mouth a few minutes later. "But you'd better start watching what you eat, and brushing after each meal."

"Wa-oog," I said, because of the cotton. I meant, "I will."

Dr. Nadler seemed to understand. I guess he's used to hearing people talk to him with their mouths full of cotton. There's probably even a course in dental school for it.

When it was finally all over, my dad picked me and my bike up. Stephanie had been right. After getting my three cavities filled, I didn't feel like going anywhere except home. I was really glad Dad had insisted on picking me up. I tried to talk to him as we drove out to Brio Drive, but my mouth wouldn't work. I couldn't form any words, and I kept drooling. It was super gross.

"Thanks, Dad," I managed to say when we got home. I opened the car door and started to get out.

"Just in case no one mentioned it to you," Dad said, "the Novocain wears off pretty quickly."

I smiled weakly. "Thanks," I said again. I knew he was trying to be supportive. Then I pushed the car door shut and trudged slowly up to the house.

Inside, I headed straight for the kitchen. I was

starving, and food always cheers me up. I had the refrigerator door open before I remembered. There was no way I could eat anything with my mouth the way it was. I slammed the refrigerator door shut and walked across the kitchen. Angrily, I yanked open the door to the basement, even though the last thing I felt like doing was working on my art project.

When I got downstairs, and saw the nearly empty bag of plaster and the ruins from all of my art failures, I suddenly couldn't take it anymore. I sank down on the cold floor and burst into tears.

"Lauren?" It was Roger. "Are you down there?"

I sniffled. "Yes," I said. My mouth was starting to work better.

"Telephone for you," he said.

I sighed as I pulled myself to my feet. "I'll be right there," I said. The way things were going, it was probably Dr. Nadler saying he'd discovered four more cavities!

"Hello?" I said, picking up the phone.

"Lauren? This is Hope. How did it go at the dentist's?" Hope asked.

"Okay," I said. "Is everyone still at your house?"

"Actually, they just left," Hope said. "They decided they couldn't wait for my dad to close the clinic. They wanted to go home so they could work on their projects."

98

I sighed. "I guess you're going to work on your project now, too."

"I do have a little work left," Hope said. "But that can wait. I thought I'd come over to your house. Like I said before, I've helped my dad put plaster casts on dogs and cats. I'm sure I could help you."

"Oh, Hope, that would be great!" I said. I'd forgotten that Hope knew about plaster casts because of her dad. It was perfect. And, if *Hope* helped me, I could still keep my new project a secret from the Sleepover Friends — particularly Kate — until the art fair.

"I could bring over some of the bandages my dad uses on animals," Hope offered. "They would make the whole job a lot easier."

"When can you come?" I asked eagerly. Having Hope's help was sounding better and better by the minute.

"Right now!" Hope said. "I'll ride my bike."

About five minutes later, the doorbell rang. Hope had a bag full of bandages with her.

"I forgot — I'm almost out of plaster," I said.

"It doesn't matter," Hope said. She pulled a little bit of the bandage stuff out of the bag and held it out for me to feel. "The plaster is already on the bandage. All you have to do is get it wet and put it in place. When it dries, you have a cast!"

I explained what I wanted to do, and Hope said, "What a great idea! I'll even be your model."

We got a pail of water and the jar of petroleum jelly. Then we went to work.

When I sat down at my desk in 5B on Wednesday, I tried to tell Kate that I was actually *done* with my art project, and it had turned out pretty good.

But Kate wouldn't let me finish a sentence. She just went on and on, telling me all about her visit to Hope's. "She's got this terrific table-top loom that her father made for her. She's also got bundles of yarn up in her attic. She makes her own dyes using wild plants she collects," Kate rattled on enthusiastically. "I think I'm going to make a video of her at work. Part of it will be Hope collecting plants. Then I'll show her making dyes from the plants and dying the yarn. Then a shot of Hope weaving. I'll end with the finished product, maybe shot from a lot of different angles while classical music plays in the background. I'll call it *Weaver at Work*. The video club will love it! It's too bad you didn't come over, Lauren." Kate finally paused for a quick breath, then added, "How was the dentist, anyway?"

I told Kate all about it. She agreed that Mrs. Kluez and Dr. Nadler would both make great characters in a horror movie. Just thinking about the weird camera angles Kate was describing for the ordeal of the drill made me shudder. It was healthy food forever as far as I was concerned. And, of course, a strict schedule of tooth-brushing and flossing.

I was about to tell Kate about my art project when the bell rang. After a quick check on how our ticket sales were coming, Mrs. Mead started right off on our math homework.

I wasn't able to bring up my project until lunchtime, when Kate asked me how it was going. I smiled. "Thanks to Hope, great! I really think I might even win a ribbon after all. I was almost ready to give up yesterday."

"Shh!" Stephanie said, cutting me off. "Be careful what you say, Lauren." Stephanie made a sideways motion with her head, and I saw that Jenny Carlin was sitting at the next table. Jenny wasn't looking our way, but it was pretty obvious she was listening to our conversation. But I was on to her now. Jenny wasn't going to find out about my latest technological breakthrough — Dr. Lenski's preplastered bandages.

"Hi, Jenny," I called to her. I chuckled when I thought about her three bags of plaster. I just knew Jenny would love knowing about those bandages!

Jenny looked over, and I gave her a friendly wave. "How is your art project coming?"

Jenny gave me a superior smile. "Just fine, thank you."

"Jenny is going to take first place in the sculpture category," Angela Kemp said confidently.

"Really?" Stephanie asked. "What did you make, anyway? It must be something really big. I mean, you were buying enough plaster the other day when I saw you. Three bags full . . . just like the nursery rhyme about the sheep."

"Baa, Baa, Baa," Mark Freedman, Henry Larkin, and the other boys at the next table bleated at Jenny.

"Very funny," Jenny said.

"What *are* you doing, Jenny?" Patti asked, trying to be nice. But Jenny wouldn't know nice if it tripped her and sat on her. Nice is just too much of an alien concept to her.

"I'm not going to tell *you* what I'm doing," Jenny sniffed, sticking her nose up in the air. "You'll find out, all right. But not until the art show on Saturday. Then losers, weepers."

Kate rolled her eyes. "Now that's an original putdown if I ever heard one," she said. "Those two really bug me. If they were on TV, I'd turn them off."

Stephanie pretended to pick up a remote control and click it at Jenny and Angela. "There," she said. "Done!"

"They don't bother me," I said. And they didn't. I didn't even care if Jenny got a blue ribbon for her sculpture, and I didn't get anything. Well, maybe I cared a little. But I'd really worked hard on my project. And, like Patti had said, I was proud of all that I'd learned in the process. For one thing, I'd learned to have a new respect for artists. Art might look easy, but take it from me, it isn't easy at all! I'd also learned that Hope is a good friend. She really *helped* me, without doing my project for me.

"Here comes Hope," Patti said.

"Let's ask her to the sleepover at Stephanie's," I suggested.

"Good idea," Stephanie agreed. So, as soon as Hope sat down, Stephanie asked her.

"I'd really like to," Hope said, "but I can't. Dad is taking Rain and me out to dinner tomorrow night at this vegetarian place he heard about that's out on the highway. It's kind of a celebration of spring. It's going to be one of our new family rituals. We used to do lots of stuff like that back in California." Then she stopped smiling for a second and looked wistful.

"Well!" Kate said brightly, changing the subject. "Has everyone sold their tickets?"

Hope nodded. "I've been selling them in the afternoons to the people who bring their pets to see my dad."

"I had to go door to door," Patti said. "But I'm sold out now."

"I still have a few to go," I admitted. "That's what I'm going to do after school today. Want to go with me, Stephanie?"

"My parents said they'd buy the seven I have left over if I baby-sit the twins this afternoon. Sorry."

"Want me to come over for a while later?" I offered. "I could help you with the twins."

"Thanks, Lauren," Stephanie said. "I'd like that. I'm sure Jeremy and Emma will, too."

"I'll come over as soon as I finish selling my tickets," I said.

Chapter
10

"Is that a bowl of your onion-soup-olive-bacon-bits-and-sour-cream dip?" Kate asked when she let me into Stephanie's playhouse Friday night.

I shook my head. "Actually, it's my new health dip." I set my overnight bag down on the floor and put the bowl of dip down on the counter.

I looked over at Patti and Stephanie sitting side-by-side on one of Stephanie's matching couches. They were hunched over a magazine.

"Aren't they even going to say hi to me?" I asked Kate as I took off my jacket.

"Probably not," said Kate. "As you can see, they're totally absorbed in that ridiculous quiz in the back of *Teen Topics*. It's the same one Stephanie wanted us to take last week." Kate lifted up the corner of the foil covering my bowl and took a peek at my new dip.

"Hey!" Kate said. "This stuff is green!"

I laughed. "Of course it is. It has avocado in it."

Stephanie looked up from the magazine and winked at me. "Remember the time we put avocado all over our faces, Kate?"

"The facial?" Kate asked. "How could I forget?"

"Bullwinkle loved it!" I said with a chuckle. "Remember how he licked our faces off for us?"

Stephanie shuddered. "That was super-gross!"

"And tonight we're following Bullwinkle's example. We're going to eat it instead of wear it." I took the rest of the foil off the bowl. "Come on, everyone. Dig in!"

Kate sighed. "Okay, I guess I'll try it. Where are the barbecue potato chips?"

Patti bolted up from the couch. "You didn't bring barbecue potato chips, did you, Lauren?"

"Of course not." I unzipped my overnight bag and pulled out another foil package. "Ta-da!" I said.

"Celery and carrots!" Kate said.

"They're great for dipping. They don't break like chips do," I said. I picked up a celery stick, dragged it through the dip, then snapped off a bite. "Delicious," I said.

Patti picked up a celery stick and dipped it. "Not bad," she said after she'd tasted it. She dipped her celery stick again. "In fact, it's great! I like it even better than your other dip, Lauren."

106

I took a little bow. "Thank you," I said.

Stephanie tried the dip. "It's good. Too bad Hope's not here. This is something I'm sure *she'd* like."

"We'll see her tomorrow at the art fair," I reminded everyone.

"I can hardly wait!" Stephanie rubbed her hands together in anticipation. She looked around the playhouse. "Do you think we should use that wall over there for our art gallery?"

"Mine will fit there," I said.

"Won't you have to set yours *on* something, Lauren?" Kate asked. "You can't put a sculpture on the wall."

"My sculpture can go either way — up or down," I said mysteriously.

"What is it?" Kate demanded.

I shook my head. "You'll find out tomorrow," I said, wagging my finger at Kate, "and not a minute sooner!"

"Lauren's right," Patti said. "We decided to wait and be surprised."

"What we need is something to take our minds off the art fair," Stephanie said.

"I know I do," Kate agreed. "Otherwise my curiosity will torture me all night."

"Get comfortable, everyone," Stephanie said, waving a carrot stick at us. "It's time to take this quiz." She sat back down on the couch with Patti and picked up the worn issue of *Teen Topics*. "Hand out the pencils and paper, Lauren," she commanded. "They're over there next to the hot-air popper."

As I did what Stephanie asked, I saw that she'd brought a hot-air popcorn popper out to the cottage. She'd also brought a blender, a toaster oven, and a bag of supplies. Just looking at the stuff made me hungry. Obviously we were going to be cooking up some snacks that night. I could hardly wait.

"These quizzes are always so silly," Kate huffed. Kate hates magazine quizzes almost as much as she hates fortune-telling and horoscopes. But she took a pencil and some paper from me anyway.

"I'm going to read the instructions," Stephanie said when I was sitting down again.

The instructions were kind of long, but they basically said we had to doodle, you know, like you doodle when you're talking on the phone or when you're supposed to be taking notes in school.

"Has everybody got it?" Stephanie asked. We said we did. It wasn't very difficult to get.

"Then start doodling!" Stephanie said. "You've got three minutes."

I usually draw faces when I doodle, so that's what I did. Sometimes I try to draw really good-looking people. Sometimes I draw silly-looking people. It depends on my mood. That night I tried to draw the best face I could.

Kate drew several lines of neat little stars. Patti drew all sorts of boxes. Then she put all her boxes in triangles. Stephanie drew women in glamorous clothes, of course. She also drew a bunch of hearts sort of sailing in the air around the women.

When we were finished, we handed our papers to Stephanie. Stephanie looked up what each doodle meant in the Doodle Dictionary. Then she cleared her throat importantly and began.

Kate's stars meant she had high aspirations, and the neat rows meant she was organized. That was no surprise! Patti's geometric shapes meant she had a mathematical, scientific mind. Stephanie's doodles meant she was obsessed by clothes and love. No news there! The results of the quiz were just too easy. For once, I had to agree with Kate.

But then Stephanie did me. According to the magazine, I was a very artistic individual who was headed for success in all my creative endeavors! My mouth fell open. Me? Lauren Hunter, art klutz? It had to be some mistake!

"Are you making that up?" I asked Stephanie suspiciously.

Stephanie handed me the magazine. "Read it for yourself."

I did, and it said exactly what Stephanie had said! I shook my head in wonder. "Have I changed in the last two weeks or what?"

"Well, you've got three fillings now that you didn't have three weeks ago," Kate said. "That's a change."

I threw a pillow at her, but she ducked and I missed. Stephanie picked it up and threw it back at me. After that I lost track of who was throwing what at whom. I do remember thinking that it was a good thing our art gallery wasn't up on Stephanie's walls yet. If it had, it probably would have been destroyed.

Saturday morning was kind of crazy. We slept later than we'd meant to, and Mrs. Green had to come out to the playhouse and wake us up. We had a quick breakfast of cereal and toast, then Mr. Green drove us home. We had to get our art projects and go back to school to set up before the judging started.

As soon as my parents dropped me off at school, I hurried to the tent. The first thing I saw was Mrs. Mead — she was there with Ms. Gilberto and several other teachers. They were helping everyone find the right spot to display their work.

"Hello, Lauren," Mrs. Mead said. She looked at my project and smiled. "That's a very interesting sculpture."

"Thank you," I said, even though I wasn't sure

if "interesting" was a compliment or not.

"Sculpture goes over there." Mrs. Mead pointed to the far corner of the tent. "You'll see the area that's been set aside for the fifth grade when you get over there."

I started across the tent. I hadn't gotten far when I saw Jenny Carlin standing in the sculpture area. I hurried over to see how her project had turned out. "Hi, Jenny," I said.

"Oh, hi, Lauren," Jenny said nervously. She looked at my sculpture, then she looked back at her own. It was a plaster face lying flat on the table like a plate. It looked kind of eerie, like a person in great pain or something.

"Is that a death mask?" I asked because it reminded me of some South American Indians we'd recently studied.

"No," Jenny snapped. "It isn't."

"Sorry," I said to Jenny's back as she huffed off.

"What's Jenny so upset about?" Stephanie asked, coming up behind me.

"Nothing, as usual," I said. Then I added, "I really like your jumpsuit." It was red and white with black trim.

"Wow! Is this your sculpture? I *like* it," Stephanie said. I could tell she really meant it. "It's not at all what I expected. I thought you were planning on doing a sculpture of a cat."

111

"You did?" I said. I was glad that I'd managed to surprise Stephanie after all. We stood and looked at my sculpture together for a minute. I couldn't help it — I was really proud of it. What I had done was cover Hope's left forearm and hand with those plaster bandages — four times. When I removed them — *carefully* — I had arranged the four arms in a square, with each hand overlapping the arm next to it. It looked pretty neat.

"Hi, you guys." It was Kate. She looked at my sculpture and said, "Oh, wow! Your sculpture is so symbolic, Lauren! It's fantastic."

"I think so, too," Patti said, joining us.

"How did you do it?" Kate asked. She bent over and examined my sculpture closely. Then she straightened up and said, "It looks like it's made with bandages, like the mummy in *The Curse of the Mummy's Crypt*!"

"It *is* bandages. Hope brought them over Tuesday afternoon. Those four arms," I said, pointing at them, "are all Hope's! She was my model."

Patti nodded thoughtfully. "It fits our friendship theme perfectly, Lauren. One arm for each of us, overlapping to say, 'all for one and one for all.' And our new friend Hope is in it because you used her arm to make it."

"But what's this next to your sculpture?" Kate asked, frowning at Jenny Carlin's piece.

112

"I'll tell you what it is," Stephanie said. "It's creepy — just like the person who made it!"

"Come on. Let's go look at everyone's projects," I suggested.

"Mine first," Stephanie cried. "Follow me." She led the way across the tent. I braced myself for a Christian LaPerle-inspired shockeroo.

"Where are we going?" Kate asked as we passed the fashion design area.

"Not here," Stephanie said mysteriously. She kept going until she'd reached fiber arts.

"Here," Stephanie said, stopping in front of a little quilt. "Do you like it?" she asked. "It's a wall hanging."

"I get it!" I said right away. "There's a square for each of us."

"Right!" Stephanie said. "This one is yours, Lauren." She pointed at a square of blue-and-purple fabric with an "L" embroidered in the corner.

"That's Bullwinkle, right?" I said, pointing at the big black dog Stephanie had painted in the middle of my square. She must have used the fabric paint she was buying at Hale's. "But why the shoe?"

"It's a *running* shoe, of course," Stephanie said.

Kate's green square had a "K" and a video camera and a plate of fudge on it. Patti's square was yellow and white. There was an embroidered "P" in the corner, and a bunch of test tubes in the middle.

113

Stephanie's square was, what else, red, white, and black! Inside her square, above the embroidered "S," Stephanie had painted all four of our faces.

"It's wonderful!" Kate said.

"Yeah," I said softly. I was really touched by the way she'd put all four of us in her quilt.

"Thanks," Stephanie said. "I'm glad everyone likes it."

"Now let's see yours, Kate," Patti said. Photography was right next to fiber arts. Kate led the way and stopped in front of a big posterlike thing.

"It's not just one picture — or even four. It's *lots* of pictures." I looked closer. "And other stuff, too."

Kate beamed. "It's a Sleepover Friends collage. Our whole history is here." She pointed to one corner where a slip of paper was glued. "This is my recipe for super-fudge. And here's one of Dad's tongue depressors." Kate and I used to use those for sticks in our homemade Kool-Pops. "And here are a few pieces of caramel corn," Kate added wistfully. Super-fudge and caramel corn were now on the list of forbidden snacks.

Stephanie pointed to one of the photos and said, "Remember that?" It was a picture of the four of us with purple goop in our hair. "That was Patti's first sleepover ever!"

"Oh, no! Kate, you didn't!" I cried when I saw

the infamous baby picture of Kate and me on the blanket in our diapers.

Kate laughed. "I had to, Lauren. It shows how the Sleepover Friends got started . . . with us." I couldn't argue with that.

"Look on the bright side," Kate added. "At least you're not alone on that blanket." That's the best part of being one of the Sleepover Friends. None of us is ever alone — at least, not for long.

"Okay," Patti said, hustling us in the other direction. "My turn." Patti had mentioned various things about her project off and on. Still, when she stopped in front of her project, I was really surprised.

"A poem?" I said.

Patti nodded. "It's a poem about friendship that I decorated with computer graphics. It's kind of like computer-generated embroidery."

As soon as Patti said that, I noticed the intricate pattern in different colors surrounding the poem. "Did you write the poem yourself?" I asked.

Patti shook her head. "It's from that little book you guys gave me when I had the flu. I thought that made it doubly perfect for our Sleepover Friends Gallery."

"Read it out loud, Patti," Kate asked.

"Okay," Patti said. "It's called 'My Friends.' " Patti took a deep breath, then she read the poem just loud enough for Stephanie, Kate, and me to hear. When she finished reading, we were all quiet for a minute. I know we were all thinking how perfectly the poem described our friendship.

Finally, Patti broke the silence. "I don't know about the rest of you," she said with a wide grin, "but I bet Lauren is starving."

"You're right!" I said. "Let's go out and see what kind of food they have at the carnival." We walked toward the opening in the tent.

"Somehow, I don't think it's going to be healthy," Kate said.

Stephanie sniffed the air. "I smell popcorn popping," she said. "And peanuts roasting."

Patti nodded. "They're both healthy snacks," she said.

"And I see cotton candy being spun," Kate said.

I grabbed Kate's sleeve and started pulling her toward the booth. "Let's go!" I cried.

Okay, okay, I *know* cotton candy isn't exactly a healthy snack. As Patti pointed out while we were paying for it, it's also called *spun sugar*. But no one can be good all the time, not even me. Besides, I'd brush well later on.

We played Pin Whistler's Mother in Her Rocker, and fished in the Art Supply Fish Pond. We had just gotten in line to throw darts at a Mona Lisa Dart Board when I spotted Ginger and Christy hurrying toward the art show tent. They each had something dangling from a hanger.

"Look!" I said, poking Stephanie in the ribs with my elbow.

"Oh, wow!" Stephanie cried when she saw them.

"They couldn't agree after all," Kate said. "Christy made an ugly blouse, and Ginger made an equally ugly pair of shorts."

"Are you kidding!" Stephanie looked at Kate in disbelief. "That's a fantastic outfit! They're *sure* to win first prize for fashion design. I'm glad I decided to make my quilt."

"First prize?" Kate sounded outraged. "Christy's blouse is a jungle print, and Ginger's shorts are *plaid*. They don't even go together!" Stephanie and I looked at each other for a second. Then we burst out laughing.

"What's so funny?" Kate demanded.

"That's the Christian LaPerle look!" Stephanie said.

Suddenly, Horace was beside us, tugging on Patti's sleeve. "Come on!" he said. "I think the judges just gave you a ribbon, Patti!"

"All right!" Kate whooped. "Let's go see."

When we got in the tent, we saw that a lot of ribbons had been given out. Patti had a red one and so did Kate. And Stephanie had gotten a blue ribbon!

"I would have been just as happy with a red," she said, picking it up and looking at it. "Maybe even happier." Natch.

"Hi, you guys!" It was Hope. She had a white ribbon, which meant her weaving had come in third. I had seen it earlier, while we were still getting set up. It was really neat — she had tied a bunch of strings between two short sticks, and then woven a sort of a landscape between them, using blue, white, yellow, and brown yarn.

Hope smiled at Stephanie and said, "Congratulations. Your quilt is terrific."

"Let's go see how you did, Lauren," Patti said.

I took a deep breath. Suddenly I felt really nervous. "I'm not sure I can stand to look. You go look for me."

"Oh, for Pete's sake," Kate said, "*I'll* go look."

"I'll go with you," Stephanie said. Patti and Hope stayed with me.

"It doesn't really matter, does it?" Patti asked.

"No," I said. Then I said, "Yes." Then I said, "I don't know. It does and it doesn't."

Kate and Stephanie came back with their hands behind their backs and sad looks on their faces.

"Sorry, Lauren," Kate said. "You only got a — "

" — blue ribbon!" Stephanie screamed, whipping it out from behind her back.

"All right, Lauren!" Patti cheered, patting me on the back. I was jumping up and down.

Hope smiled. "It really was a great idea, Lauren."

"It only worked because you helped me," I told her.

Hope shrugged. "What are friends for?"

"Well, that takes care of our trophy case," Kate said. She sounded satisfied.

Stephanie started counting — "One, two, three!" And we all said, "Sleepover Friends Forever!"

SLEEPOVER FRIENDS

#34 Kate the Winner!

"Kate, it's a good thing you won six tickets to Wilderness World in the raffle, so we can all go!" Stephanie said. She, Patti, and I all jumped up and down.

"But wait — six isn't enough, Steph," Lauren interrupted our celebration. "It's only enough for Mr. and Mrs. Beekman, Kate, Melissa, and two other Sleepover Friends." We all stopped and stared at each other.

I could hardly face Patti, Lauren, and Stephanie. How could I tell one of them she couldn't come to Wilderness World? How could I possibly choose?

SLEEPOVER FRIENDS™

by Susan Saunders

Available wherever you buy books...or use this order form.

THE BABY-SITTERS Club®

Collect Them All!

by Ann M. Martin

The seven girls at Stoneybrook Middle School get into all kinds of adventures...with school, boys, and, of course, baby-sitting!

For a complete listing of all the Baby-sitter Club titles write to:
Customer Service at the address below.

Available wherever you buy books...or use this order form.